EMILY SILVER

TRAVELIN' HOOSIER BOOKS

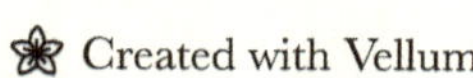 Created with Vellum

Thank you so much for reading Reckless Royal! I have taken some literary license when writing this book in regard to the Succession to the Crown Act, passed in 2013. Prior to 2011, any second-born male could displace an older sister in line to the throne. Since this is my own royal world, this does not apply in this book.

Happy reading!

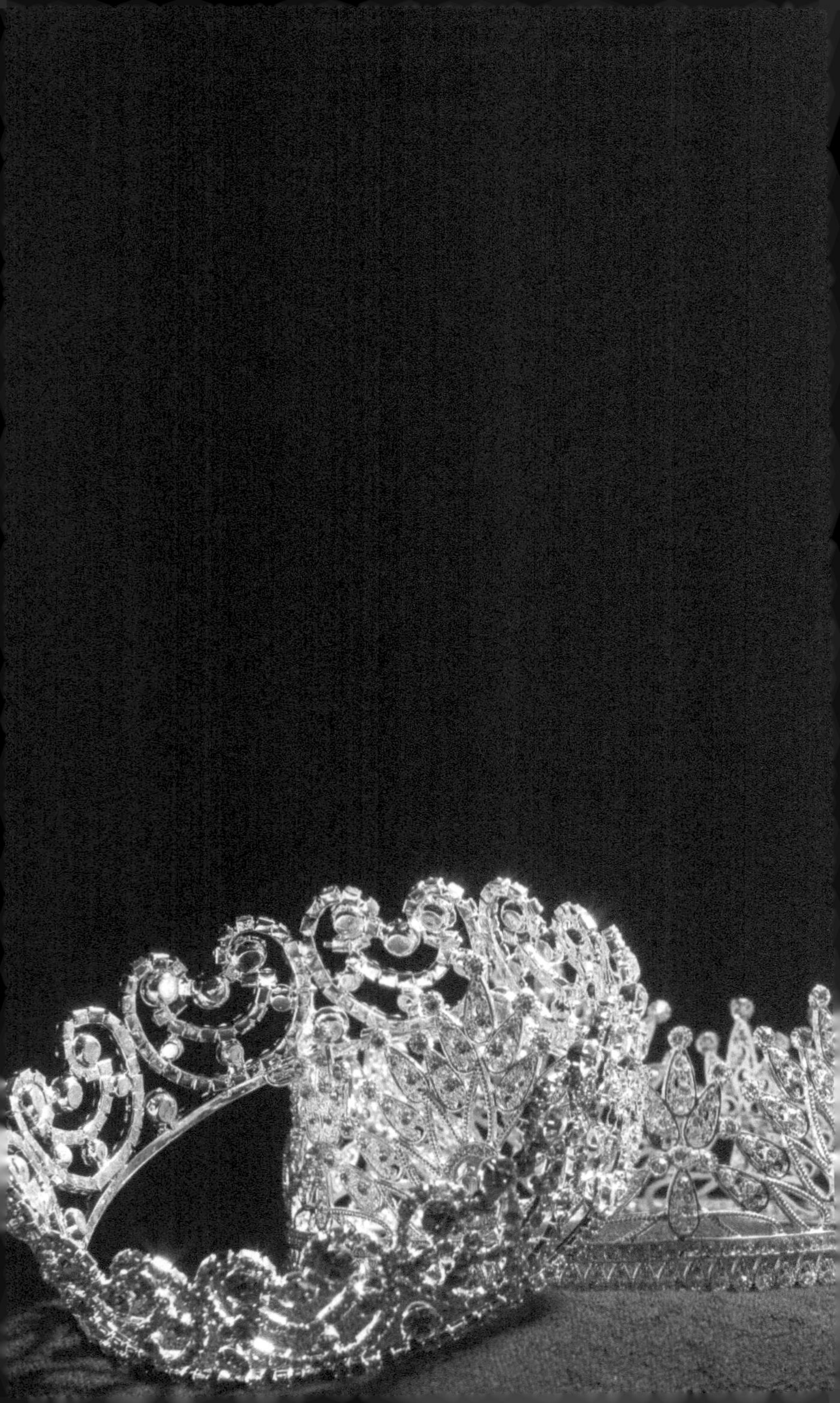

Chapter One

JAMES

"**C**an you think with anything besides your prick, James?" Bloody hell, I'm in for it now. I can't help it if the paparazzi are leaking old photos of me. Even if this one is awful. I'm getting sucked off in a club. You can't see anything inappropriate, but anyone with half a brain knows what's going on.

"The Queen will be over to have a word with you shortly. This is out of my hands." For fuck's sake. It's never good when the Queen has to get involved.

"I'll be sure to let her know it won't happen again."

My advisor, Charles, gives me an appraising look. His bushy white eyebrows are furrowed. I'm sure I've given him wrinkles early in life. I can't help it if I like to have fun.

"Will it, though? This isn't the first time we've seen this happen, and I doubt it will be the last. You're first in line to the throne now. This behaviour is unbecoming of the future King."

"You don't need to remind me of my position in life." My voice is harsh as I snap back at him. Ever since my twin renounced her spot in the royal line, all eyes have been on me. Before, my behaviour was considered cute. That of a playboy prince sowing his oats. Now, everyone has turned on me.

"Someone needs to." That voice sends people scurrying to stand and bow. It's still strange seeing Mum as the Queen. I stand, buttoning my blazer as I do. "You all can leave. I'd like a moment with my son."

My advisor and his staff exit on a bow. Cowards. Leaving me here to fend for myself. Heading to the tea cart, I pour us each a cuppa.

"Thank you, darling."

I take a sip, eyeing her with suspicion. "To what do I owe the pleasure of this visit, Mum?"

"As if you don't already know." She sits on the velvet loveseat in my office. Everything here is velvet. Quite annoying really, considering I'm the future King and it's decorated for an old grandmum.

"Why don't you enlighten me?" I can't help the cheekiness in my voice.

Mum sets her cup down on the coffee table in a huff. "James, this has to stop. You are almost thirty now. You can't keep expecting people to excuse this behaviour."

"It's amazing how quickly they turned on me."

She pinches the bridge of her nose. Mum's hair was always a dark brown like mine, but now there's more grey peppered in. It gives her a regal air. But today, it's just pissing me off.

"If you don't start making some changes, and soon, I'll be forced to take action."

"You'll be forced to take action? What the bloody hell does that even mean?" My voice carries as I push off the loveseat. "I don't need you controlling my life." Shoving my hands through my hair, I try to take a calming breath.

"You have yet to prove to me that you are capable of

taking on even the smallest of duties that I was doing for your grandfather when I was your age. You are just not ready to be King." Her voice becomes quiet as she mentions him. He died almost a year ago, but it still hurts to think about him. He was one of the best Kings England has ever seen, and I know Mum is doing everything in her power to live up to his standard.

"Maybe if you'd actually give me those duties to do, I could try. Have you ever thought of that?" My hands on my hips, I stare Mum down. I hate being questioned like this. "I'm already being held to an impossible standard."

I know I've hit a sore spot when Mum rolls her eyes. "An impossible standard? You were allowed to run around with no regard to the crown and get away with it. Your sister was held to an impossible standard and look where that got us."

"That was below the belt." Ellie hated everything about royal life. The media. The people commenting on her every move and appearance. She's much happier living as a private citizen, but damn, if that doesn't hurt.

"It's true. You need to be held accountable, James. And it's going to start right now." She pushes off of her seat and goes to leave.

"What do you mean 'it's going to start right now'?"

"I am not getting any younger, James. This position has a way of aging you before you're ready. Dad did everything he could to prepare Eleanor for the crown, but now, I'm afraid I must do the same for you."

"Mum. I'll do better. I promise."

She opens the door to leave. "Until you show me that, then I'll continue with my own plans."

Fucking hell.

THE MUSIC IS TOO loud tonight. Club Mayfair has always been my favourite. I get special treatment here. All the free drinks, sexy women fawning all over me, and no press allowed inside. The scotch is doing little to quell my nerves. A blonde is sitting by my side, her dangerously long nails trailing up and down my thigh. It's doing little to arouse me tonight.

I'd be all for a quick romp in the sack with her, but right now, Mum's words keep playing on a loop in my head.

Not ready to be King.

How does one even prepare to be King? It's not like I haven't been paying attention all these years. Sure, I've been more concerned with women, but I still know what it takes to run a country. Or at least I think I do.

"You want to get out of here, Prince James?" Any attraction I might have had to this woman goes down the toilet at those last two words. I know most women are with me because of who I am, but I can't handle it tonight.

"Sorry…" Bloody hell, I can't even remember her name. "I'm just not feeling it tonight."

I nod to my Personal Protection Officers, my PPOs, that I'm ready to leave. It's still early, so hopefully I can pop over and see the one person who might actually be able to talk some sense into me.

"Are we heading home, Your Highness?" my security officer asks, as I dodge the questions of the paparazzi that are awaiting my exit before getting in the idling car.

"Head to Ellie's, please." I throw my blazer over the backseat and close my eyes. Why is this shite bothering me even more today? Maybe because it's coming from Mum. It's my advisors who are the ones to condemn me for my behaviour. Never has Mum gotten involved before.

"Shall I call ahead and let her know that we are coming?"

"Please do. Otherwise, she may be irritated."

The car lurches into the street as the noise of the club fades away. I'm hoping my sister will be a voice of reason. For being this early in the evening, it's a quick drive through the city. When we pass through the gated entry of Ellie's neighbourhood, I release a breath.

"Thanks, guys. I won't be long." I hop out of the car, seeing Ellie at the front door. Her once brown hair is now pink, a stark contrast to mine.

"Why the hell are you coming over to my place at nine at night when you could be out at the clubs?" She waves me in as I kiss her cheek.

"No Sean tonight?" My sister's face softens at the mention of her partner, Sean. If she hadn't stumbled into his tattoo parlour when she ran away from the palace, I don't know where I'd be right now. That's a slippery slope to go down.

"He had a session run late. What's brought you over here?"

I flop down on her couch, rubbing my eyes. "Mum. The palace. You name it."

She messes around in the kitchen before returning to the living room. "I'm guessing it has to do with that picture that is spread all over the news?" She hands me a scotch before sitting in a chair next to me.

"You saw it too?" Christ, I didn't think she'd be looking at tabloids once she left the royal life behind.

"It's hard not to hear it from the parents when they're whispering about me at the school." Ellie took the reins of

Sean's after school art programme and helped build it into what it is today. She keeps it running on the days that Sean is at his tattoo parlour. I don't know how they manage both, but they love it.

"Hopefully you didn't see it." I shiver, taking a long pull of the scotch.

"Absolutely not! I wouldn't go out looking for that. But it serves you right for getting caught. It's not like you were ever discreet with your women."

"Thanks, Ellie. Just what I needed tonight." My eyes roll on their own.

"Why are you so morose tonight? Couldn't find anyone to take home at the club?"

"Is that really all people think I do?" Shite, maybe Mum does have a point.

"Jamie. It's all you lead people to believe. There're no photos of you going to galas or art show openings or state dinners because you're always going out with women. It takes precedence over anything else you might do."

"Fecking hell. You sound just like Mum." I shake my head. "But you may have a solid point."

"Is the world ending?" she asks on a gasp. "I don't think I've ever heard you say those words to me before."

"Alright, alright. Quit being a smart arse."

The front door opens with a bang as Sean races in. "Is everything okay in here?" He looks haggard. "Oh, hey, James. What are you doing here? I thought something happened."

"Other than me being a prick, nothing going on."

Sean walks over and drops a kiss on Ellie's head. I can't be bitter towards my sister. She was not cut out for royal life. Seeing her this happy, starting her own family, makes me realize I do need to step up and take responsibility for myself.

I gulp down the rest of my scotch and drop it on the table behind me. "Thanks, Ellie. You've been a big help."

She looks confused. "You don't have to leave now that Sean is home. Are you going to be okay?" Her voice sounds concerned. She worries about me more than she should.

"I'll be fine. You just helped me see a few things more clearly."

Ellie gives me a wary look. "If you're sure." She walks over to give me a hug as I head out.

"See you later, Sean."

"Always a pleasure, James." He waves me off as I jog down the stairs.

I just need a plan to present to Mum. Maybe she'll see reason if I start to take control of my life. As much as it pains me to admit, even cutting the club visits in half would be a good start. I may be the prince, but I'm by no means a saint.

Chapter Two

"Lord Kendall. Thank you so much for meeting with me today."

"Your Majesty. It's such a pleasure to meet you. Please, call me Xavier." The duke bows, his bald head shining bright towards me. One of the perks of being the Queen. If I need to take action, people are at my beck and call.

"Please, have a seat. Would you care for some tea?"

"That sounds delightful, Ma'am." I ring the bell next to me, my indication to the wait staff to bring it in.

"Please, call me Katherine."

"Katherine, then. What summons me to the palace today?"

As the tea is prepared, I drop my hands in my lap, a position that has been engrained in my head since I was a girl.

"Here you are, Your Majesty." I take the cup, giving my butler a grateful nod.

"Xavier, I was hoping that you and I could come to an arrangement of sorts."

"An arrangement? What kind of arrangement are you thinking of?" His brows furrow in confusion.

"I know finances have been a bit hard for you lately."

"I'm sorry, but how is that any of your business?" He sets his cup down, as if he's about ready to walk out. No one walks out on the Queen.

"My apologies, Xavier. But I'm merely stating facts that are public record as a duke. We are both in a position where we can help each other out."

"And how is that, Your Majesty?" I don't miss the extra emphasis on my title.

"My son needs stability. You need money. I believe your daughter is around my James's age, yes?"

He gives a sharp nod. "What are you getting at?"

"An arranged marriage." I hold his gaze. There's a slight tick in his jaw.

"With your son? The 'playboy prince'?" He winces this time, giving me an apologetic look. "Sorry. I'm sure he's a fine young man, but with everything the press runs with, all I see is his long line of women."

"I agree. He's had little direction in his life until this point. He was always going to be second in line for the throne, so he was never held to any sort of standard. And I'm afraid much of that is my fault. But now, he needs to get serious about his position. And I don't see that happening."

"Unless he has a woman on his arm."

"Precisely. And your Zara is unattached."

Xavier gives me a firm look. I can see he's fighting himself. He doesn't want to agree to this plan, but he also can't say no to the Queen. The latter part is what I'm hoping for.

"It will ensure your financial future." The perk of being a royal is that we have deep pockets. And I'm not above using personal funds at this moment to benefit the entire kingdom. "James has it in him to be one of the best Kings this country has ever seen, but he needs a steady hand at his side."

"And you think my Zara is that steady hand?" Xavier sips his tea.

"Yes, I do. There is no mention of her in the press, she teaches at a good school, and comes from a respectable, steady line."

"I didn't know our family line would be called into question," Xavier states firmly, setting his cup down.

"No one is calling your family line into question. You come from a good background, and we would be lucky to have someone of Zara's calibre in our family to carry on the Ainsworth line."

"Ahh, yes. The heir and the spare."

I bristle at his remark. "We don't call our children that."

"Isn't it what will be required of them?" He raises an eyebrow at me in challenge.

"While there are certain expectations to carry on the line, they are not simply the heir and the spare."

"And what will the expectations of Zara be?" He leans back, crossing his arms.

"While we cannot guarantee they will be scandal free —because the paparazzi publish what they want—I don't want to see Zara plastered over the news falling out of a nightclub or being caught in any compromising positions."

"My Zara is better than that."

I give him a slight nod of my head. "She seems like a fine young woman. Someone who will be an asset to our country. She'll also be required to be a patron of some of our more established royal charities but can also establish one of her choosing."

"And of course, the royal offspring."

"Yes, bearing children will also be required."

"When will you need an answer?" He stands, awaiting my dismissal.

"I'm sure I'll hear from you soon. Lord Kendall, it was a pleasure having you here this afternoon." I extend my hand. He takes my hand willingly, even if he might not agree with what I'm proposing today.

"Your Majesty. I'll be in touch." He bows before leaving the room.

"Your Majesty, can we expect to set up the tea for next weekend as originally planned?" My advisor is at my shoulder the moment he leaves.

"Please do. I am positive he will say yes."

"And Prince James?"

"Cancel anything he has planned and make sure his advisors are aware he is not to be late. Best set the appointment for an hour earlier for him to ensure he's here on time."

I love my son more than words can describe, but it's time I take his future into my own hands. For his own good, and the future of this country.

Chapter Three

ZARA

"Everyone's practised, yes?" Looking around, I see nervous faces staring back at me. Never a good sign.

"Okay then. Ready." I raise my baton and instruments are readied. I move my hands on memory alone as the students start playing. Notes are missed, strings aren't tuned, and the beauty of the song is lost. It takes everything I have not to stop the song immediately and dole out criticism. Their lack of practise is evident.

As the song ends, I take a deep breath, steeling my face. "Sounds like we could use some work on that song."

"It was bloody awful, Miss Cross," one of the students pipes up from the back.

I fight to keep my face straight as murmurs of agreement break out. "Not your best work, no. But since it's a Friday, let's see if we can clean it up a bit and then we'll break out the pop songs."

"Yes!" A chorus of cheers go up around me. Nothing like pop music over the classics to motivate a group of secondary students.

"Alright, alright. Still need to make it through

Beethoven." This time, when they start playing, it actually sounds like the famous overture.

As I'm passing out the sheet music for the new song, the final bell of the day rings.

"Okay, since we didn't get to this today, practise over the next two days, and we'll play it Monday. Have a lovely weekend."

Students gather their bags as they head out for the weekend. "Bye, Miss Cross. See you Monday," is called out by many as they leave, and I wave in return. Planning next week's music for our end-of-term concert can wait until Monday.

What I've really wanted to do all day is work on my own piece. Music has been a part of me for as long as I can remember. As much as I love it, teaching was a more stable career choice. And as the daughter of a duke, I was expected to have a stable career.

Picking up my own prized violin, I tune the well-loved instrument. It's my most cherished possession. The one my mum used to play daily. I get my love of music from her. If only she could see me now.

Pulling out the sheet music, I start playing the song I've been writing over the past few months. The beginning is fine, the middle okay, and the end terrible. I've been stuck and can't seem to find a breakthrough.

"This is all wrong!" I mutter to myself, dropping my bow. The melody is there, in my head, but I can't seem to grasp onto the fading notes. It's been this way for weeks. I've always been able to write my own music, but lately, there's a block. One that I haven't been able to push past.

"How did I know I could find you in here?" My best friend's voice rings throughout the quiet studio that is my classroom. Students are long gone.

"Because I'm driving myself crazy trying to get this

piece out?" Marnie's at my side, pulling my violin from my hands.

"You do realize it's not going to come by forcing it out, right?" She has a point, but it doesn't mean I'll listen.

"I thought it was coming today." I blow out a breath, looking at the messy pages in front of me. "It's no use. It's never going to come." I crumple the sheets up in anger and toss them in the bin behind me.

"Not with that negative attitude."

"Then I'm *positive* that it will never come." I give her my cheekiest smile.

"Okay. We're leaving and hitting the pub tonight."

"Do we have to?" I love Marnie to bits. We met my first day at the conservatory where we teach and have been friends ever since. She loves the London nightlife, while I'd prefer a night in with friends.

"Don't pout those lips at me, Zara. You owe me a night out since you bailed on quiz night." Damn. I forgot about that. I was sulking over this piece, yet again, that I can't seem to write.

"First round is on you."

She beams back at me. "If it means you're coming out, I'll gladly buy."

"SO HAVE you found any good matches yet?" Marnie's words are hard to hear over the loud noise of the bar. It seems half of London is out tonight.

"If I get one more dick pic, I might scream." Marnie was in a low point after her most recent boyfriend dumped her. After too much wine one night, she somehow convinced me to sign up for an online dating site with her. Safety in numbers, right?

"Nothing worth taking for a ride?" She waggles her eyebrows in my direction.

"I've seen better." She tips her drink in my direction, as I sip on my gin and tonic, not hiding my grin. "Honestly, is this really the best London has to offer?"

"We should move to Sweden. All broad-shouldered hunks of men. I think you'd be hard-pressed to find an unattractive Swede."

"You cannot move to Sweden and ditch me here!" I slap her arm. "Who would rescue me from these endless dates I keep going on because of you?"

She lets out a sigh. "If only Prince James could just fall into my lap, I'd be set for life."

"You and every other eligible woman in London." I roll my eyes. "I'm surprised you'd want the 'playboy prince.' Last I saw, some poor woman had her hands down his pants."

"I wonder how big it is. You think he's overcompensating?" Marnie wiggles her pinkie in front of me, and a snort of laughter escapes.

"Of course he is!" I cry. "Women are only with him because he's the prince."

"You do have to admit he is attractive. Probably knows how to please a woman too."

"Only because he's been with so many. Honestly, Marnie, I thought you had better taste in men," I chuckle. "The prince is so not your type."

She nods her head at me. "I need someone girthier. He'd snap like a twig under me." Marnie has curves and knows how to flaunt them. She can bring down any man she chooses, if only she could find the right one.

"I'd settle for anyone who can go more than two

seconds without looking straight past me." I'm tall and straight as a board, so there's not much to look at.

"If it makes you feel better, I don't stare at your chest when I'm talking to you." She winks at me.

"So much better." I finish the rest of my drink. "As much fun as it is bemoaning our nonexistent dating life, I need to get going. I have an appointment with my dad tomorrow afternoon."

"What are you helping your dad with?" Marnie gives me a questioning look.

"Not sure. He rang me up this week and told me he'd be picking me up early, as we would need to spend the day together."

She tips her head at me. "That sounds rather ominous."

I shrug my shoulders. "Nothing out of the norm."

She drops a few pounds on the table as we walk outside. "I'm glad I got you out for a night. See you Monday?"

"See you Monday." I drop a kiss on her cheek and head into the warm, spring night. London in the spring-time is my favourite. The city comes alive after being cooped up during the winter.

It's a short walk home to my townhouse. It's been in our family for generations, seeing as how my father is one of the handful of remaining dukes in the country.

Walking into my house, waves of exhaustion roll over me. Teaching is no easy profession. I love my students, and I love my music, but this week has taken its toll. Between students not wanting to learn and fighting this block I have, I'm ready for the weekend.

"ZARA? WHERE ARE YOU?" I hear my dad puttering around downstairs as I put the finishing touches on my makeup. He was rather vague as to where we'd be going today, so I went with a plain black dress. Nothing fancy, but easy enough to fit in with any crowd.

"Coming, Dad," I shout down the stairs, before spritzing on perfume and joining him.

"Morning, darling." Dad gives me a peck on the cheek. "Sorry for being so secretive about where we're headed today."

"And where might we be going?" I grab my jacket and purse as we head out the door.

"Buckingham Palace. We have a meeting with the Queen." His brow pulls tight as he says this.

"The Queen? Why would you not tell me we're meeting the Queen? I look like I'm going to a convent!"

Dad waves me off. "You look fine. I don't think anyone will pay any mind to what you're wearing."

"But I will."

"Too late now. We best be going. I don't want to keep the Queen waiting." Disdain laces his tone.

"Why do you sound upset about meeting the Queen? Isn't it an honour to meet her?"

He rolls his eyes before opening my door to his car. "Some things aren't all they're cracked up to be. Now, let's get this over with."

"What aren't you telling me?" He starts the car and pulls out into early London traffic.

"Just know, I love you very much, darling."

"Why do I feel like I'm off to the dungeons instead of a meeting with the Queen?"

"Don't be dramatic. You'll be fine."

Easy for him to say. He knows why we're going to the palace. Between his cagey looks and his tense posture, it feels like I'm being led straight to the dungeons with no warning as to what is to come.

Chapter Four

JAMES

"Again, why are we having tea today?" Lounging on the loveseat, I lament being at the palace today. My diary was all set for the day before this unplanned event with Mum. I had a visit to a new hospital wing on my calendar but was told that it was going to be rescheduled. What the Queen wants, the Queen gets. And my new plan of action is going to have to wait another day.

"James. Might you appear more proper? You look like you're hanging out in a club."

"I can't help it if you're keeping me in the dark about what we're doing." It's hard to keep the contempt from my voice. After the other day, this must be part of Mum's plan.

I stand, pacing the small space in her sitting room. "I'm taking your words to heart, Mum. I have a plan to do better."

She's staring out the window to the back gardens. It's a grey, rainy day. "And what is your plan, my dear?" She turns a stern eye on me.

Shite. I should've known she would ask me this. After

our little chat, I knew I needed to do better. But I hadn't gotten that far.

"More charity work. Fewer clubs."

"That's your plan? We're far worse off than I thought."

"Your Majesty. Your guests have arrived." The announcement draws my attention away from Mum. Anger is boiling just below the surface like a volcano. I'm ready to erupt when a portly man with a bushy moustache enters the room. Behind him is a willowy brunette, long hair flowing around a simple black dress.

"Lord Kendall. Lady Zara. I'm quite pleased you could join us today." She tips her head in his direction, as he bows before her. Mum addresses Zara with the appropriate title of a duke's daughter. I'm wary of what this means.

"Your Majesty. The honour is all mine."

"James, this is Lord Xavier Cross, Duke of Kendall." Mum extends her hand in his direction.

The man bows to me, the woman following. "Your Royal Highness. It's always a pleasure to be in your presence. May I present my daughter, Miss Zara Cross." He motions to the woman behind him.

"Zara. I'm thrilled you could join us today."

"Your Majesty. The pleasure is all mine." As she curtsies to Mum, this poor woman's face is equally as confused as mine. Hers does hold less contempt than mine, however.

"Zara, it's nice to meet you." I try to grab her attention, but her eyes keep flitting around the room. If you've never been to the palace, it's easy to be distracted by the glamour of it all.

"Please, come have some tea." Mum motions to the small table set up in the sitting room. An unsettled feeling starts to come over me. I don't know what's going on today, but I can't imagine it will be in my favour.

"Thank you, Ma'am." This delicate woman accepts a

cup and sits. I take the empty seat next to her. Stretching out my legs, I lean back in the chair, drinking my own cup. The harsh look from Mum tells me she isn't pleased. That makes two of us. She straightens, setting her tea down.

"I'm sure you two are wondering why we've brought you here today." Zara gives me a look, only a small one. "The duke and I have entered into an arrangement."

Oh feck. This can't be good. "And what sort of arrangement is that?"

"An arranged marriage for the two of you." Her voice is curt as she drops the bomb.

"Are you fecking kidding me?" Outrage drips from my voice as I explode out of my seat.

"James! Where are your manners?"

"Oh yes, I'm sorry. Where are my manners when you've just told me I'm to marry a complete stranger!" I throw my hands up in the air. There's no beating around the bush with Mum. She came right out with why she brought me here today. Zara's staring up at me, shock written all over her face. "One typically doesn't hear of arranged marriages in this modern age."

"Zara, I apologize for my son."

"Your Majesty, may I ask the reason for such an arrangement?" At least Zara has better manners than I.

"Yes, my dear." Mum is so composed; it just further angers me. "James, can you please sit?"

I have half a mind to refuse, but it will only drive home Mum's point that I'm not ready to be King.

"James needs a wife. One that is fit to be Queen." Zara's eyes go wide, mirroring my own. "You will be the perfect match for James."

"And do I not get a say in my own life? In finding my own wife?" My words are harsh.

"Are you able to make sound decisions with the kingdom in mind?"

It would not do well to get into a pissing match with the Queen, but every fibre of my being is itching with disdain right now. An arranged marriage? "We're not in the nineteenth century anymore. I think we're both perfectly capable of making our own decisions." Anger drips from my voice.

"But why me? I'm sure there are hundreds of eligible women." Zara's voice carries the shock that I feel, but I can't help turning my anger on her.

"I'm sorry, eligible women? What is this, an eighteenth-century courtship ball?"

"Sorry to offend you, but this is rather sudden." She pins me with a glare. At least she's not falling at my feet. I'd be more concerned if she were. "I'm trying to wrap my head around all of this."

"Rather sudden? Do you know anyone whose parents have found them their future partner?" I'm not doing well to keep my annoyance to myself, as evidenced by the glare from my mother. It's hard to be concerned with her right now.

"Your Highness. There is no reason to raise your voice to my daughter." Lord Kendall turns his grey eyes on me. What kind of person promises his daughter to someone in this day and age? Only someone who isn't in the position to refuse the Queen.

"I'm sorry, but I can't be here." I move to leave, ignoring the voices calling me back. This day has taken a turn for the worse. Does Mum really think an arranged marriage will make me fall in line?

Zara

"ZARA, dear. I'm very sorry for my son. He hasn't been himself lately." The Queen is stunned at the departure of her son. I can't say I blame him. An arranged marriage? I was supposed to be teaching lessons today, but instead, my entire future has been decided for me. Shock and anger are fighting for control in my head. Why on earth would Dad do something like this?

"It's quite alright. Not the sort of news any person expects to hear, I'm guessing." I sip my tea, not making eye contact with either the Queen or my dad. When Dad said we were meeting with the Queen, I didn't know what to make of it. I certainly didn't think it'd be an arranged marriage.

"Xavier, all of the arrangements will be made. I think a spring wedding would be ideal. That would give the country time to get to know Zara."

The country? Getting to know me? Even though my father is a duke, I've never been one to enjoy the spotlight. I like staying behind the scenes while my students shine.

"Don't you think this fall will be better? Make the press think they've been together longer than just meeting now." Dad runs his hands over his moustache. "I think that would be better."

"Fall it is then. I shall have my advisors meet with you, and Zara, you too, to make plans."

"A fall wedding? Can a royal wedding be planned in only six months?"

A fall wedding. To the future King. An arranged marriage. My head is spinning.

"What about my students? What about my job? Will I have to move into the palace?" Questions burst out of me before I can grab onto them. I don't think I've ever been so overwhelmed in my life.

"There will be plenty of time to sort that out, darling." The Queen is cavalier in her response. Easy for her to say. Her whole life wasn't changed in a matter of mere minutes.

"Will you please excuse me? I need some fresh air. This is all quite a bit to take in." I stand, giving the Queen her curtsy, as required.

"The gardens are at your disposal. Take a left, and at the bottom of the stairs, go straight until you see the garden doors." The Queen is polite in her response. "Don't worry, Zara. Everything will work out."

"Thank you, Ma'am."

Once I'm out of the sitting room, I follow her directions to the formal gardens in back of the palace. The rain has died down a bit since we arrived. Spotting a gazebo, I run in that direction, but not before slamming into a solid mass.

"Oof. I'm so sorry." My hands are on the most solid chest I've ever felt.

"Zara. Did they send you out to find me?" James's disgust is now aimed at me.

"Your Highness, please. I am just as shocked by this as you are."

"Call me James. I am to be your husband after all." I wince at that. Husband. I'm going to have a husband. A husband that I met a mere thirty minutes ago. Sure, I've known my whole life who James is. It's hard not to when you grow up with the royals surrounding you at every turn.

But to marry this man? He was just plastered all over the news with his latest woman. What makes Dad and the Queen think he'll actually settle down?

"They did not send me out here to find you. I needed some air. I can assure you, this came as just as much of a surprise to me as it did to you." My voice is quiet as the rain falls softly around us.

"Christ, come on." His warm hand slides down my arm, pulling me in the direction I was heading. The patter of rain on the roof is a welcome distraction. "I'm sorry for going off back there. It's just a shock for me." James's hands are pulling on his hair. Objectively, he's quite handsome. Thick, dark hair. Bright, blue eyes. He's tall—taller even than I am in my heels, which is not the norm. And from what I felt earlier, he must work out quite regularly to have such a strong physique.

"Is this all because of the photos that leaked?"

He pierces me with a punishing stare. I can see how this stubborn man always gets his way. It doesn't faze me. I'm used to these pleading looks from my students.

"Yes. My mother doesn't seem to think I'm fit to be King." He leans against the railing, crossing his thick arms over his chest.

"And how is one determined to be fit to be King? Is there an exam?"

A smile cracks his full lips. "You haven't heard? One must play polo, learn how to smile and wave the proper way, and know the waltz to dance at the ball. All boxes that must be checked before one is proclaimed King."

"It's the polo playing you're having trouble with?"

I don't try to hide my smile as he barks out a laugh. "Quite cheeky, aren't you?"

"Just trying to wrap my head around everything that's going on today. It's a bit much." My eyes grow wide at what I just said. "I'm so sorry. I don't mean that you're too much. It's just, I've never been promised to someone before." That sounds terrible. Are we promised to one another? "I'm mucking this all up."

"It's alright." James walks over, rubbing his arms up and down mine. It's meant to be soothing, but it just grates on me. I'm supposed to convince the world I'm in love with the prince? "I mean, if I can prove to them I can do this, they won't actually make us get married next year, right?"

Even he doesn't believe that. "Hate to burst your bubble, but they're talking about a fall wedding."

"A fall wedding?" The words explode out of him. "You're fecking with me, aren't you?"

I shake my head. "Somehow Dad seems to think that it would be more believable, like we've known each other longer than a few months."

"Bloody hell. How in the world did it come to this?" The words are whispered, meant for just himself.

Nerves are rolling off him in waves. It's setting me on edge. I don't want to be here any more than he does, but this is the unfortunate situation we're now in. I have no idea what possessed my dad to agree to such a thing, but just the thought has me fuming.

"I know you don't want to be in this situation any more than I do, but this is going to be our new reality. We might as well try and make the best of it."

James turns his blue eyes on me. They're heated. I shouldn't like the intensity I see there, but I do.

"And how do you suggest we make the best of it?" Sarcasm hangs on every word.

"I'm sorry if this wasn't your idea. It wasn't mine either!" I snap at him. "You're acting like a petulant child. No wonder your mummy had to come up with such a drastic plan."

His shoulders sag with regret. "I'm sorry, Zara. I'm really not handling this well." That's an understatement. He drags his hand down his face, jaw stubbled with scruff. "I had this grand plan of what I was going to do to show Mum I was ready to take over the throne."

"That's just it, though. Why are you showing her you're ready now? It's not like you'll be taking over the reins tomorrow. You're thinking too big. You need to pull back."

This time, James gives me a pensive look. "How would I do that? Think smaller?"

"Based on the fact that they are marrying you off, instead of trying to rewrite your entire personality, show people you can do the work. Focus on the charities that you have. No one's expecting you to take over tomorrow."

James walks over to me. Even though I'm eye level with his chin, his presence looms large. Like any good future King should.

"Zara, I believe this is the start of a beautiful rela-tionship."

Chapter Five

ZARA

"I'm sorry, you're what?" Thank God, Marnie hadn't taken a sip of her wine, otherwise she would've spit it all over me.

"Promised to the Prince of the United Kingdom." I sip my own wine.

"To Prince James. The Playboy Prince."

I wince. "Can we please not call him that?"

"Is the future Mr. Zara Cross better?"

I throw my head in my hands. "Of course it isn't! I am betrothed to the prince!"

"Technically betrothed to be betrothed."

I pierce Marnie with my most menacing stare. "You are not helping this situation."

"How would you like my assistance then? Tell you he's a one-woman kind of man and will fall madly in love with you and have lots and lots of babies?"

A sickening thought hits me. "Oh God. I'll have to have two at least. Isn't it the whole thing with the spare and the heir?"

Marnie spins her finger at me. "Other way around, love."

"Marnie! I'm being serious. My children will rule this country one day." I slam my head down on the table.

"But at least you'll have very cute children." Marnie gives me a shove in the shoulder.

"I'll be in the spotlight for the rest of my natural born life. I'm going to be sick."

Marnie gulps down the rest of the wine she's drinking. "Are you even supposed to be telling me this? This seems like something that the palace would forbid."

"I told them you were nonnegotiable. I can't have this big secret and not tell you. I'd go crazy."

I turn my head to see Marnie staring at me. "I'm glad I'm included in the need-to-know people."

"I just can't believe my dad did this to me! I mean, what was he thinking?" Maybe if I picked up any of his numerous phone calls this last week, I'd know. But I'm too angry with him to think straight.

"Why didn't you say no then?"

"Could you say no to the Queen? She has this air about her." I wave my hands around me. "She's the Queen. You can't say no to her. It was a done deal before I even walked into the room."

"While I know I should be mad on your behalf, can I also be excited?"

As much as this whole situation is wearing on me, Marnie's reaction makes it a little lighter. "I guess. You'll get to attend all the events for the wedding too."

Marnie's eyes sparkle at this news. "I'll have to be sure I get the best fascinator in town. No one can upstage the best friend."

"I'm glad you're thinking big picture here."

"They said fall wedding?" I nod in response to her

question. "It'll be absolutely gorgeous. Your dark hair, with a fur wrap walking into Westminster Abbey? I can practically see it now."

I've lost her. Details were fuzzy at best, but the royal wedding was to happen within the next six months. I'd get some say, but most details were to be left to the royal staff. I was never a little girl who dreamed of her own wedding. My mum passed when I was little, so I hardly remember her. I was so passionate about music, having that connection to her, that nothing else mattered.

But now? The thought of not getting to plan my own wedding or have my mum by my side has me itching to plan the entire thing myself.

"What kind of dress will you get? Just think, everything you wear now will be sold out in minutes."

"You've officially lost maid of honour duties."

"I'm going to be your maid of honour?" She looks shocked.

"Right up until that comment about the dress."

"Bugger off, you. You're no fun." Marnie smirks at me.

"Okay, Marnie. I love you, but time to go." I wave my hands towards the door. Trying to absorb everything that will happen in the next few months is not easing my nerves.

"Zara, for real." Marnie grabs my hands, pulling me up and into a hug. "Everything will work out. You have more grace and poise than anyone I've ever met. If there's anyone who would be a worthy Queen, it'd be you."

The annoyance I felt just moments ago fades. "Fine. Maid of honour status reinstated."

"Yes!" She pumps her fist. "Trust me, Zara. Things always work out the way they should. I mean, how many people can say they were talking about bedding the prince and then he just falls in their lap."

"Pretty sure that was you saying that." I shake my head as she makes her way to the door.

"Well, at least now we'll know for sure."

I let out a sigh. My patience is nonexistent right now. "Know what?"

Marnie winks as she shouts over her shoulder, "If he's really overcompensating."

Chapter Six

JAMES

This is already going to be a nightmare. I'm twelve years old again, my mum setting me up on play dates. Except this time, it's with the woman who is going to be my future bride. But not that I have any say in it. I mean, if I become the prince Mum wants me to be, she won't make me go through with this, right? I'll just play by their rules until I can come up with a plan to end this whole charade. Which means playing nice with Zara.

I'm meeting her at a posh club for dinner and drinks. I offered to pick her up, but she insisted on meeting me here, no doubt to cut out early if she wants. Fine by me. I can head to the club after. Shite. I'm not supposed to be doing that. I need to prove to Mum that I am fit to be King. And hopefully not be tied down to this woman. Based on her first impression, I can't imagine she wants me.

Arriving at the club, I notice a few paparazzi lingering about. That should help get the buzz out about Zara and me being together. The more believable this is, the better.

Flashbulbs pop as I enter the dark club. Cherry wood walls make it darker. Old gas lamps on the walls give it a sexy feel. Adjusting to the change in light, I spot Zara at a cosy booth in the back. Zara, with her long brown hair, big doe eyes, and deep red lips, has an understated sexiness to her. She's quiet but has quite a bit of cheek to her.

"Zara. Lovely to see you this evening."

She stays where she is. "Nice to see you too."

I unbutton my blazer and take a seat. This is going to be much harder than I thought. She fidgets in her seat. It's clear to anyone passing by she doesn't want to be here.

"Your Highness. It's lovely to have you here tonight. Can I get you your usual?" our waitress asks as Zara's eyes are perusing the menu.

"How about a bottle of the house red?" I give her a wink as she struts away, a little sway in her hips. Swinging my gaze back to Zara, I'm busted.

"I know you like your women, but if we're to make this work, you'll need to at least appear to be interested in only me." She goes right back to the menu. Damn, if this woman isn't going to keep me on my toes.

"My apologies." The waitress chooses this moment to drop off our wine. As she pours our glasses, she bends over, trying to get me to look down her shirt. Instead, Zara's gaze locks with mine. A smirk plays on her lips as our waitress walks away.

"Cheers." I clink my glass with Zara's, drinking more than is considered polite.

"So, James. Have you thought anymore about the predicament we find ourselves in?"

Zara is quite the lady. Her lips close around the glass of wine, taking a demure sip. The image of her on her knees, sucking my dick, pops into my head. Bloody hell, I need to get my head in the game. I can't be attracted to the woman that is supposed to be my fiancée.

"Like you said, maybe if I start small, I can convince

Mum that I'm fit to be King. Maybe then they'll put an end to all of this nonsense. I mean really, an arranged marriage?" I try to keep my voice quiet, but I'm annoyed. I've been annoyed since the moment I left that blasted tea last week.

Zara nods along. "And how do you think they'll take not planning a royal wedding?"

"We'll convince them we want a long courtship and a long engagement. People do that these days, right?"

"I hate to point out the obvious, but seeing as how I've never been married, I can't comment." She smirks at me behind her wine glass.

"Otherwise you wouldn't be here. It's considered blasphemous if a royal marries someone who's been divorced."

"Probably because they aren't a virgin."

I choke on the sip of wine I just took, thankful I didn't spew it everywhere. Where in the world did this woman come from?

"Your Highness. What will it be for dinner?" The waitress bats her eyes at me, completely ignoring Zara.

"Zara?" I tip my head in her direction. She gives her order to the waitress, a knowing smile on her face. I give her mine and dismiss her.

"Will this be my new normal? My very existence being ignored?" She waves a hand in the direction our waitress went in.

"For now? Yes."

"Way to sugar-coat it." Zara rolls her eyes, taking a sip of wine.

"Zara." I cover her hand on the table with mine. "It's a hard life. But once they realize who you are to me, you'll wish for anonymity."

"I guess I should be thankful then." Her voice is quiet now.

"Enough about that. Tell me about yourself, oh future bride of mine."

She rests her chin in her hand. Her brown eyes cut into me, flecks of gold sparkling at me. "Let's see. I'm twenty-nine, teach music at a local conservatory, and am newly betrothed." She wiggles her eyebrows.

"Are you always this cheeky?"

"Apparently you bring it out in me."

I give her my most winning smile. "That's not what I usually bring out in people."

"I'm well aware." Zara's eyes are anywhere but on me.

"Something wrong?" Her eyes zip to mine. She looks nervous now.

"Sorry. I just feel like all eyes are on us in here."

The room is relatively dark. The club is meant for privacy inside, but wandering eyes are always glancing around to see who is here.

"It comes with the territory. You'll get used to it." I take a long draw on my scotch.

"Will I though? I haven't the first clue as to what I'm supposed to do in this role."

Zara's fingers are playing with the napkin on the table. She's nervous. Of me or what she's gotten herself into, I don't know. Reaching over, I still her hand with mine. Zara's tall, but her delicate hands fit perfectly under mine. It's a bit jarring how perfectly my hand holds hers.

"It's not as if you'll be thrown into the role of Queen tomorrow. I won't hang you out to dry all on your own." I give her hand a squeeze.

"That's oddly reassuring."

"Well, I have been doing this my whole life."

"Seems like your mum might think otherwise." Zara gives me a soft smile behind her wine glass.

"Coming out with the big guns, I see." Our food gets

dropped off, and I notice Zara once again being ignored by the waitstaff.

"So, what's the best part of being royal?" she asks, cutting into her food.

"The best part of being royal?" I don't think anyone has ever asked me that. Sure, people always assume it's being in the spotlight, but to be honest, I've never thought about it.

"There are some days where I feel like I'm helping people. Not just doing it in name only, but really helping them."

"And here I thought you were going to say the women."

"My reputation precedes me." Even Zara thinks I'm a ladies' man. Can't say I blame her. If the only thing she knows about me is what's written in the press, then that's all she'd know.

"I know people don't take me seriously, but I want to do a good job. I want to find something that I can put my name behind and believe in. We have this event next week, at one of the national museums—"

"We do?" Zara cuts me off.

"Best get used to your life being planned out to the minute."

"Sounds lovely." She rolls her eyes at me, going back to her dinner.

"You get used to it. This event next week is for the British Arts. It was something Ellie always supported, and it's now fallen on me. I'm fine supporting the arts, but it's not my calling."

Zara studies me, her eyes penetrating my own protection shields. "You're different than I thought you'd be."

"I'm hoping good different."

"I like that you don't want to just take what is given to

you. You are striving to be better. To make a name for yourself. I can't imagine how difficult that must be in your position. Especially considering why I'm here."

"Where in the world did you come from?" I ask on a laugh, trying to diffuse the tension coiling inside my chest.

"I'm serious, James. It must be so hard being raised in the spotlight and everyone thinking you're one person, and then having to be someone completely different."

"I'm glad you see it that way." I give her a soft smile. This conversation got much heavier than first date conversations should get. But I guess that's what happens when you're dating your future wife.

Chapter Seven

"Miss Cross, are you dating the prince?" one of my students pipes up in the back. We're working on a new piece today, but they've been badgering me all day after seeing the pictures of James and me leaving the restaurant the other night.

"If you keep asking, I won't give you our new song to play today."

Their moaning isn't held back.

"I don't want to play more Vivaldi!"

"Ugh, dead music is so boring!"

"Alright, alright. If you give me your very best for the next thirty minutes, we can switch back to the newer pieces next week."

Cheers go up around me. I tap my baton and twenty students straighten, readying their instruments. Waving my hands, the music swells around me. As much as my students whine, they are brilliant performers. The music takes over, and I'm swept away. My eyes close as I lean into the motion. It's familiar. Soothing. It doesn't matter what is going on outside this room. Music is in my soul.

As we hit the crescendo, and then the music quiets, I come back to the room. Focused faces are drawn tight as the piece ends.

"That was absolutely brilliant. Well done. I'll have the new music ready for tomorrow. You've earned it!" I clap my hands, signalling to them they can put away their instruments.

"Can it be Beyoncé? I really want it to be Beyoncé!"

"I'll make a note of that, Eugenie. Now get going. Have a nice evening, everyone."

Cases shutting and chatter from the students are the last sounds for the day. It's been an exhausting few days, and I can't wait to get home. This weekend is another planned outing with James. The few paparazzi that were outside the club ate up our appearance together. James said with a few more outings like that, we'll be established as a couple. I try not to let the thought make me sick.

I hate the limelight. James loves it. I guess you have to be comfortable in the spotlight when you grow up with cameras being shoved in your face. James has a natural rapport with them. I hope I develop a thick skin. They won't be easy to deal with.

Packing up, I lock up my room and make the short walk to my house. I love Hammersmith. It's quiet. You don't feel like you're in the hustle and bustle of London. Slinging my violin higher on my shoulder, I turn onto my street. There's a commotion down the street. Getting closer, my nerves start tingling. They can't be in front of my house, can they?

"Zara! Zara! Over here!"

My worst fears are confirmed as cameras are shoved in my face. One paparazzo turns into five, which turns into ten. Where in the world are they coming from?

They're surrounding me on all sides.

"Zara, are you sleeping with the prince?"

"What's James like in bed?"

"Will you be the future Queen?"

I'm being pushed from side to side. A violent shove from behind sends my bag skidding across the sidewalk. Everything is flying out. Bending over, I try to scoop it all up when it happens in quick succession. A camera gets shoved right in my face, throwing me to the side. I can't focus on the jolt of pain, because my violin is next to hit the ground. The crunching sound of the bag over the crowd is crushing.

"No!" The initial shock has worn off as I start to push my way through. "Back up, you vultures!" Grabbing the case, the tinkle of wood stings my heart. My most prized possession is likely damaged beyond repair. Shoving everything in my purse, I hurry to the security of my house. Thank God for the gate.

The chaos behind me fades away as my trembling hands unlock the door and I rush inside. Tears prick my eyes. Setting my violin down with all the care in the world, I grab my phone and dial James.

He answers on the first ring. "Hey there, fiancée."

"J-James?" I stutter, not hiding the panic in my voice.

"Zara. Are you alright?" All lightness in his tone is gone. "Is everything okay?"

"No. There were paparazzi waiting for me at my house."

"I'll be right there." He hangs up before I can get another word in.

Looking in the mirror, an angry red cut mars my cheek. What in the world will the students think tomorrow?

Hot tears stream down my face. It's a struggle to catch my breath as I collapse into the safety of my sofa. How in the world did they find me? The house isn't listed in my name. Will I have to fight my way through them every day now? Will I have any privacy anymore? Panicked thoughts race through my head as the commotion outside hits a new high.

A pounding on my door has me hiding behind the wall. Are they able to get on private property? Aren't there laws against this?

"Zara? Open up. It's James." Rushing to the door, I confirm it's him and pull the door open, hiding behind it.

"Are you alright?" He pulls me into his arms, but not before I see his security officers escorting the paparazzi away.

I only shake my head, my throat clogged with emotions. I squeeze him tighter to me. The spicy scent of his cologne soothes my frazzled nerves. If I could burrow into his arms, I'd stay here.

His hands smoothing my hair back is calming. The stubble on his neck is scratchy, grounding me.

"What happened, Zara?" He pulls back, cupping my face. Anger churns in his eyes.

I walk away, seeing my violin case. My heart is in a vise as I open the case. "I was walking home from school, and they were there. I don't know how there were so many of them on me all at once, but I couldn't get away. They were shoving me, and then they knocked my purse and violin out of my hands."

My stomach drops to my feet as I see the damage done. My most prized possession is broken. My mum's violin. One of the few memories I have of my mum is her playing for me on this violin. And now it's shards of wood and string tangled together. James's warm hand is on my shoulder.

"Can we fix it?"

I slam the lid shut. "No! We cannot fix it!" Rage is

coursing through my veins. "It is a custom-made violin from California. You cannot fix it! It was a wedding gift from my dad to my mum. I don't know if they even make these anymore." The tears won't stop. Forget the ache in my face. The ache in my heart is splitting me in two.

"I'll make this right. I don't know how, but please, Zara, let me help."

I stalk away from him, heading through the short hallway into the dining area. I need a drink. Pulling off the stopper, I take a swig of scotch, wincing as it goes down. I have it for when Dad comes to visit. But tonight? Tonight, it's needed.

"I thought I'd have more time." I'm staring down into the crystal bottle. Did my life just become public fodder for the entire world to see? Sure, my students knowing is one thing. But I'm not quite prepared for billions of people to know my name.

"I'm so sorry, Zara." The heat of James's body is behind me as I take another hit of the scotch. "Okay, if you don't slow down, I'll be carrying you to bed." James grabs the bottle from my hand, setting it down behind me. "I usually like a woman to be sober when I take her to bed for the first time."

He tries to break the tension settling over me. It does little to quell the racing thoughts in my head.

"How am I going to navigate my life? Will they be out there all the time now?" I wave towards the window.

"I've already called Mum and made the request for you to have security officers with you at all times." He brings his hand up, stopping me before I can interrupt. "I know you won't like them, but I can't have anything happening to you."

"Right, because it'd be terrible if your fiancée were to be hurt." I roll my eyes.

"Stop it, Zara." His voice is firm. The hands on his hips tell me now is not the time to argue, but feck it, I'm in a fighting mood.

"This isn't a love match. We're not in love. Why are you so upset by the truth?"

"Just because we're not a love match doesn't mean I want to see you get hurt! I'd have to be pretty cruel to leave you to the wolves." His voice rises with anger.

"They are terrible, aren't they?" James's anger on my behalf takes the fight out of me. "Will it always be this bad?"

"The press can be great when things are going well. But when there is a scandal? Forget about it."

"So, every day of your life then?" I give him a playful smile. My nerves are settling. I can't think about my violin, or the anger will return.

"Ouch. I like this cheeky side of you, Z." My cheeks pink at the nickname. I've never let anyone call me Z before. But when James does it? I quite like it.

"What can I say? I guess I'm feisty when I'm tossed around." That takes the laughter right out of him.

"Can I take a look at your face?" He touches my cheek where it stings.

"Sure." I'm tired. A headache is forming, and the adrenaline from the day is fading.

James's hands are gentle on my face. "Got a plaster? You're bleeding a bit."

"Really?" I rush to the mirror, and sure enough, blood is caked on the small cut under my eye. Grabbing James by the elbow, I direct him to the half bath at the end of the hall.

"Pop up." He pats the counter and I do as he says. He's focused on the task at hand, digging out the plasters from the first aid kit.

I wince from the pain as he dabs antiseptic on the cut. "Ouch! Is that really necessary?" He takes my face in his hands, blowing gently on the cut. I'm starting to like the feel of his hands on me.

"You don't want an infection." His eyes bore into mine. He's ready to fight me on this. I give a subtle nod, allowing him to continue.

"Besides, maybe this will give you some street cred with your students."

I grab his hand, dodging his touch. "Have you ever met a music student before? I think I would get more street cred if I met the conductor of the London Symphony Orchestra."

"And here I thought I was one of the cool kids," James says on a laugh.

"I'm pretty sure everyone tells you you're one of the cool kids just so they don't hurt your feelings. That or they want to meet the Queen."

"Wow. So much for progress." His touch is light as he puts the plaster on my cheek. I hate to admit it, but it really does feel better now. James drops his hands on either side of me on the counter. We're at eye level.

James has some of the most expressive eyes I've ever seen. They really are the windows to his soul. Whatever he's feeling, you can see it in his eyes. His blue eyes are dark now, fighting a storm of emotions.

"Zara. I know this wasn't in your plan. I'm dragging you through the weeds, just to change the world's view of the 'playboy prince.' If it's too much, you have to tell me now. Fuck whatever agreement our parents have. If you can't handle this, say the word."

The kindness in his eyes settles me. I made a promise to him. I hate going back on my promises. Aside from that disastrous first meeting at the palace, James has shown me nothing but compassion.

"Whatever your decision, I'll respect it. If you want to walk away, I'll respect that. I know this isn't what you signed up for," he says as he cups my cheeks.

The heat from his touch is new. Not like the other times he touched me tonight. No.

This feeling is new.

The butterflies are new.

The need to taste his lips is new.

And it's frightening. James is a womanizer. He didn't get the nickname Playboy Prince because he's a saint. More like a sinner. I can't have feelings for this man. Feelings are dangerous.

His breath ghosts my cheek, heightening the sensations coursing through me. "But if we do this, I will do everything in my power to keep you safe. I know what the world thinks of me, but I promise, I'll do everything I can to shield you from the paparazzi." The sincerity and vulnerability in his voice solidifies my decision.

Taking a deep breath, I clasp his wrists. His pulse is racing. Could he be just as affected by me as I am by him?

"We're in this together, James. There's no going back now."

Chapter Eight

Our date last week went better than I thought it would. Zara couldn't be more different than the woman I first met with at the palace. The woman at the palace was hesitant, uncertain. But the Zara I'm meeting now is lively. Maybe it had to do with the fact that she got herself tied to the "playboy prince" and is responsible for helping clean up my image.

"So, have you bedded your future wife?" Oliver's voice breaks me from my thoughts.

"Are you serious with this shite right now?" I look over at my oldest friend who has his long blond hair pulled back into a bun. He's always trying to impress the ladies and appear more rocker than his Cambridge upbringing would care to suggest.

"I'm just messing with you. Christ, this woman has already got your knickers in a twist."

I flip him off, taking a long pull of my drink. "The whole point of this is to prove to everyone that I'm ready to be King. If I bed her, as you say, that would be the exact opposite of what I'm trying to prove."

"And how long do you plan to keep this up?"

"What do you mean how long? It's a done deal."

He gives me a cheeky look. "Come off it. You mean there's no way that you can get out of an arranged marriage?"

"Would you want to cross my mum?" I give him a knowing look. Even when we were little, one cutting look from her and we'd fall in line.

"Fair point. So, you're just going to marry some woman you don't even know?"

"Ahh, that's where you're wrong. They were trying to rush us, but now they're giving us until the fall to date and get to know one another before they announce the engagement. I'll know everything there is to know about my future wife by then."

"I've seen you take longer to decide where you want to eat dinner. There's no way you'll know enough about this woman by the fall." Even in the dark club, I can see anger tighten his face. "I can't believe you're going along with this."

"It's not like I have any choice." Bitterness laces my voice. "This is the last thing I wanted. But there's no other option since Ellie fled."

"How is she doing, by the way?"

"Pregnant." As unexpected as it was, I'm quite looking forward to being an uncle.

"No shite. Missed the train on that one."

"Oy! She's quite happy as she is, so you can feck off." Oliver wasn't the only one of my friends I had to fend off Ellie. It seemed all my friends wanted to date her when we were growing up. One of the downsides to having a twin sister.

"Alright, alright." He throws his hands up in defeat. "I wasn't serious. But good to know she's doing well."

"Part of why Mum wants me to settle down. No one is going to take me seriously as the King if I can't keep it in my pants."

He snorts over the drink he just took. "Did she actually say that to you?"

I shake my head. "She didn't, but my advisors did. Talk about an awkward conversation."

"Shouldn't you be used to everyone talking about your dick?"

"And on that happy note, I need to get going. I have to pick Zara up for another event this evening."

"Wow, they're not wasting any time." Oliver stands, clapping me on the back.

"What can I say? True love waits for no man."

Zara

IT'S ONLY BEEN a few days since our first date, and my weeks are already planned out for the next three months. There are no fewer than three events each week to ensure maximum exposure for the two of us. It's exhausting to even think about.

After dinner the other night, James and I walked out together. While there were only a few paparazzi around, it was enough. They've been following me every day since to and from school. Thank God for the security officers, or I don't know what I would do.

Tonight, they'll be swarming. It makes me uncomfortable to think about that many people snapping my picture because of whom I'm with.

Because of the early hour of the event, James is picking me up straight from school. I did a quick change in the bathroom and am trying to calm my nerves before he gets here. I'm glad the students have already left, otherwise it would be even more of a spectacle. The press has been stationed outside the school since they found me.

Nerves surge through me as James's motorcade rolls to a stop in front of the school. I was fine with meeting him at the event, but he wouldn't have it.

"My future Queen." James's deep voice washes over me as he steps out of the car. If I wasn't so upset about this situation my dad had pulled me into, I could appreciate what a gorgeous man James is. I'm not noticing how good James looks in his suit, or how his irises disappear as he gazes at me. I changed into a simple grey cocktail dress with a lace overlay, hitting me at my knees. I'm trying not to notice how goose pimples break out as his eyes blaze a hot trail over my body.

"My future King." I accept the double-cheek kiss as he waves me into the awaiting car. "And what does tonight's event entail? You were rather secretive."

"Tonight's benefit is for the national museum to raise funds for a new exhibit on British history. People tend to be fast and loose with their money if you feed them more alcohol."

"I'll have to add that to the list of things I need to remember."

He shrugs, giving me a playful smile. "That's why we're not in charge of the planning. There are people much smarter than us who know these things and plan accordingly. We're not much more than pretty faces."

"And is this one of your new charities that you're taking on?"

James does a good job of hiding his nerves about his new place in the royal line. But underneath all the bravado of this man lies someone who really doesn't want to mess up in his new role. I can't imagine the kind of pressure he's under.

"It's one Mum reassigned to me. Not my favourite by any means. Ellie was much more into the arts than I have ever been."

"Are you able to find something that you're passionate about?" I don't have the first clue about how royals come by their patronages, so I can't really offer much in the way of support.

"Sometimes yes, sometimes no. There are the charities that, historically, we've always supported that we will continue to do so. But sometimes there are new ones that we can get behind as long as it's a sound investment."

"And what will my charities be once I'm in the fold?" I observe the long line of press as we get to the museum.

"We'll worry about that later. Are you ready to wine and dine everyone tonight?" James waggles his eyebrows at me.

"As ready as I'll ever be." I didn't expect to be thrown into the deep end so soon. I thought there would be more of a learning curve, but here we are.

The flashbulbs are bright as the car door opens and James steps out. Taking a deep breath, I slide out behind him and take his awaiting hand, holding on for dear life.

"James! James! Over here!" James gives the person yelling his name a big smile. I'm not sure how he can distinguish him from the rest of them. "How did you and Zara meet?"

I shouldn't be surprised that they already know who I

am. I can only force a smile as James tells them our fake story about us meeting through mutual friends. They eat up his every word. James is a natural at this. He has an easy grace that makes him perfect for the role he was born into.

"Zara. How does it feel to be dating the prince?"

James pulls me closer to his side as I try to formulate an answer. I knew there would be press here tonight, I just didn't think we'd be stopping to chat with them. But I guess it's all part of the palace's plan to rehab James's public persona.

"James really is a prince." *Really is a prince?* I want to die on the spot. James squeezes me closer as a playful look lights up his face.

"You certainly seem to have charmed him."

"That she has. Now, if you'll excuse us. Have a nice evening, everyone." James is polite in his dismissal as he pulls me towards the museum entrance.

"Glad to know I really am a prince." His hot breath ghosts my ear, sending butterflies through my stomach.

"Shut it. I completely blanked on anything even remotely normal to say." I give him a hard shove in the stomach, but he doesn't move an inch.

"I guess we'll just have to work on that then." The jest in his eyes gives way to something else. Something almost like lust and longing. But that can't be possible, right? We were thrust into the most unlikely of situations and have only known each other a short time.

"Prince James. Lady Zara. How lovely of the two of you to join us this evening."

An older man wearing a pinstripe suit and an oversized moustache greets us at the door.

"Dr. Sharpe. It's a pleasure to see you again. May I introduce you to Lady Zara Cross?"

"It's a pleasure. I am so happy the two of you could join us this evening." Excitement is dripping from every pore as he leads us into the crowded museum. "All of the exhibits are open. Wine and cocktails are being served, so if you have any questions, please do not hesitate to let me know." He bows as he backs away from us.

A server walks by with a tray of champagne, and James grabs two, one for each of us. "To a night of fun." He winks at me before clinking his glass against mine.

"Cheers."

"So, care to work the room with me?" James gives me his arm as we mingle amongst the guests.

"How many of these people do you actually know?" Being the daughter of a duke, I recognise certain faces, but everyone's face tonight is a blur. It's the first official event the two of us are attending together. Trying to put my best foot forward is even more nerve-wracking than I thought it would be. One false move, and we'll both be making head-lines tomorrow.

"I know a lot of them, but a lot are new. Take that guy." James points in the direction of a tall, older man with a young woman on his arm. "That's his third wife, I believe. Could be number four. He's always a good person to chat up. Likes people to know he has money and will spend it."

It's hard to hear a word of what James is saying because "—you can't get past her tits, right?" James finishes my thought for me.

"I mean, would you look at those?" My voice is a loud whisper as I take in the woman's appearance. "They can't be real. They're like two water balloons!"

"Shh, you don't want anyone to hear you. We can't be judging the people we're trying to schmooze." His voice is filled with laughter as he takes me in that direction.

"Prince James! Who is this gorgeous woman on your arm?" asks the gentleman as we approach. The woman with him shoots me a menacing glare.

"Lord Paxton. This is Zara Cross. You may know her father, the Duke of Kendall?" Lord Paxton gives me an appraising look.

"Ahh, yes. How is the duke doing these days?"

"He's quite well, thank you." I tip my head in his direction.

"Splendid to hear. It's nice to see you young folks supporting such a marvellous cause. One can never get enough of our own history."

"The National Museum has always been a cause near and dear to my heart." James is so full of shit, yet this portly man is hanging on his every word. James's eyes are sparkling with amusement as they carry on their conversation. The young woman pays me no mind. It's just as well. I should get used to being invisible.

"Yes, well, I'll be sure to match my donation from last year. I don't want to keep you. I'm sure everyone wants to meet this beauty on your arm." Lord Paxton bows low in our direction, as an uneasy feeling washes over me.

"Do they always make you feel so slimy?" I whisper to James as we walk away.

"Those old men? Yes. I don't see him often, so at least there's that."

"Thank goodness for that."

James stops and pulls me into a small alcove, hidden from the eyes of onlookers.

"Are you uncomfortable being here?" His eyes hold mine captive.

"Not uncomfortable. It is just different than I thought it would be." It's hard to explain. "That man seemed to look right through me, yet was also looking at me like he wanted to make me his next wife."

"Well rest assured, you're no one's wife but mine." His smile is dazzling, bright white teeth standing out in the dark corner, as he moves in closer to me, caging me in.

"Doesn't that sound medieval?" I poke him in his hard chest.

"Your dad and my mum arranging our marriage is medieval. I can't help it if that means that no one else gets to look at you like that."

This protectiveness shouldn't be as captivating as it is. And yet, I'm finding myself completely taken with this man.

"Well, it could be worse." I shrug my shoulder. "You could be with Miss Tits back there and suffocate anytime she tried to cuddle with you."

Laughter bursts out of James, and I muffle my own in the crook of his neck. That spicy scent of his is intoxicating.

"God, I can't even imagine. He probably bought them for her."

"I'm telling you right now." I grab him by the chin, looking into his bright blue eyes. Eyes that I can get lost in. "I am never getting anything like that. I may not be well-endowed, but I would topple over if I had those."

The air is sucked dry around us as James goes quiet. His gaze is so focused on my face, as if he's trying to ignore the area of my body I just pointed out. His tongue darts out, licking that full bottom lip of his. I bet it would taste like the champagne we've been sipping on. What I wouldn't give to suck that bottom lip into my mouth and taste him.

"We should probably get back out there. We don't want

people to think we've already ditched the party." His voice is rough, filled with a need I feel down to my toes.

I take a settling breath, trying to recalibrate after this heated moment with James. "Right, fundraiser. A prince's work is never done."

Chapter Nine

JAMES

I'm all over the place. For the last two weeks, I've been fighting all of my emotions for Zara. I was raging at Mum for setting us up. It's the twenty-first century. Why are arranged marriages still a thing?

Then I was annoyed at Mum for finding Zara. She could have found someone that I didn't like to make it easier to stay mad at her. But no. The woman I'm coming to know now is full of zest. Full of life.

And fecking hell, if that isn't making me crazy. When she called me after the paparazzi attacked her outside her house, it took everything in me not to wring their necks. Instead of running, she doubled down on this crazy life with me, even if it means having a camera constantly shoved in her face.

It's a fact of life. The paparazzi will do anything to get a shot of us. Especially if it's in a compromising position. But when they hurt someone who's been out with me one time? Rage. White-hot rage that I've never felt before. It meant that I couldn't keep my hands off Zara at the fundraiser last night. It was like if I wasn't touching her, she would disappear. I liked having her by my side. She was winning people over like I could only hope to.

I shouldn't want more from her. I can't want any more from her. I can't destroy her life any more than I already have. Sure, she says she's all in. But in this life? The paparazzi already following her every move? Already attacking her once? I hate to think of what else could happen to her.

My sweet, music-loving fiancée.

She doesn't even know how sexy she is. How sensual. Fecking hell, I'm getting hard again just thinking about her. It's been a struggle to push thoughts of her out of my head, but after a long day, I give in.

Taking my dick in my hand, I free him from his cotton prison. Just the thought of Zara has me ready to explode. Imagining it's Zara's nimble fingers and hot mouth on me, I give a few hard strokes and am close to coming. Those pouty lips of hers would know exactly how to suck me off. It'd be better than some nobody doing it in the back of a club, just for the need to get off. She'd look up at me with those big doe eyes, and bloody hell, I'm coming harder than I have in a long time. *Faster* than I have in a long time.

Feck. I'm covered in cum. Stripping off my shirt, I clean myself up before finding a new pair of boxers. I shouldn't be jacking off to thoughts of Zara, but damn, this woman is crawling under my skin no matter how hard I try to fight it. I'm just going to have to try harder.

IT'S the day of the Royal Flower Show, and it's going to be teeming with press. The Royal Flower Show was always Ellie's event. But now, it has been passed off to me. Another duty I have to show that I'm fit to handle.

Standing at Zara's door, I smooth my hands over the lapels of my jacket and ring the bell. I'm nervous. I can't remember the last time I was nervous to take a woman out. But when Zara opens the door and ushers me in, all thoughts flee my brain.

Feck. What did I say about trying harder to not be attracted to her? She's wearing a white jumpsuit that shows off all her curves, and her hair curls around her shoulders. She's beautiful.

"Zara. You look incredible." I kiss each cheek, breathing in her sweet scent. She's radiant, and I can't seem to stop staring at her.

"You look quite dashing yourself, James." My khaki trousers and navy blazer are an easy outfit for an official, yet casual, event. Everyone always tries harder to make the flower show a fancier event than it really is.

"Are you ready to woo your citizens?" Shite, why am I acting like Granddad? No one says woo these days. What is it about this woman that drives me mad?

"As I'll ever be." She takes my proffered arm, and I lead her out of the house. Her hand on my arm tenses as we make our way to the car. The paparazzi are now confined to the other side of the street, thankfully, which means we can get in and out of her house without being swarmed. Sure, this moment will be splashed across headlines tomorrow, but at least I don't have to worry about a camera being shoved right in Zara's face.

"You're doing beautifully, Z."

She gives me a shy smile as my PPO opens the door for

us. "So, is there anything I need to know about today?" she asks once we're settled in the car.

"Other than oohing and aahing over a lot of flowers, no. Since I took over the patronage midseason, we didn't do a stall. That will come next year."

"Fawning over flowers, I can do that." She nods her head, twisting her hands in her lap.

"I promise, you'll do great." I grab her hands, and they still under my touch. Her gaze is fixed on them. Running my thumb over her knuckles, I try to be as reassuring as possible.

"You're a caring person, Zara. This will be easy for you. You connect with people without even trying." Her eyes flit to mine.

"How could you possibly know that?"

"Because I pay attention. Because after you came with me to the museum fundraiser, you had everyone eating out of the palm of your hand. They couldn't get enough of you." She blushes. The same blush I imagine on her cheeks when I'm making her come. Christ, these are not the thoughts I need to be having right now.

"Thank you, James. That means a lot coming from you."

"What can I say? There's a lot more to me than just the 'playboy prince.'"

PRESS ARE CRAWLING at the arrivals gate. We've slowed to a stop as it's time to get out.

"You've got this, Z. I promise." I give her hands a reassuring squeeze as the door is opened. Everyone is immediately calling for our attention. Zara has a death grip on my hand. I pull her closer to me. I want to wrap her in a bubble and not let the outside world touch this beautiful woman attached to my arm.

"Your Royal Highness. Lady Zara. It's a pleasure to have you both here today. I'm Olivia and I'll be your host for the day." Olivia bows before me, then takes Zara's extended hand. Flashbulbs continue to pop as we meet our guide for the day. I'm used to the press being at every event, but it seems like lately there are more than usual. Maybe because Zara is a novelty, and they want to catch every moment of our budding relationship.

"It's a pleasure to meet you, Olivia. I've never had the opportunity to come to the Royal Flower Show." Zara is kind to everyone she meets, regardless of how nervous she is right now.

"Well, I'm thrilled I'll be showing you around." She takes us deep into the hall, skylights overhead bright with the spring sun. Any nerves Zara had seem to have faded with Olivia's welcome. She drops my hand, and I can only follow. It's rare when my presence is overlooked. It's a new feeling, something I'm not quite used to.

"So, Olivia. What's your favourite part of the show this year?" The perfume of the flowers should be overwhelming, but it's not.

"The orchid farm. You'll have to visit. It's stunning. We also have a beautiful set of instruments made entirely from plants that I think you'll enjoy, Zara." Olivia is paying me no mind. She is absolutely taken with Zara.

Zara grabs her arm as excited eyes find mine. "You must take us there. It sounds wonderful."

"Please, this way." Olivia extends her hand, and Zara

follows her, a little extra pep in her step. It's nice to see after the stressful few weeks she's had. I find my thoughts drifting to her more and more during the day. She didn't mind the security officers I assigned to her, but trying to get her to take a car to work proved more difficult. She's quite stubborn.

Zara stops suddenly, her eyes wide. The music installation is directly in front of us.

"Olivia, please excuse us," I say to our host. She bows to me and scurries away.

"I have no words." Zara's voice is quiet. Her eyes are everywhere, observing the life-size instruments in this part of the grounds. Violins and pianos made of greenery have flowers flowing out of them. It's something straight out of a fantasy novel. Zara is walking around, touching everything in sight. Her chocolate-brown eyes are unblinking.

"You like these, then?"

She hooks her arm in mine, pulling me close, her head resting on my shoulder. "This really is incredible. I know you have to do these kinds of events all the time, but the beauty and creativity these artists put into their work? I love being able to witness it firsthand."

"You've never been here before?" Her fingers are dancing over the pieces. Her head shakes on my shoulder.

"Dad never brought me. I was usually too involved with my music and couldn't be pulled away. But seeing these, I wish I had come."

My chest swells with Zara on my arm. Where did this woman come from? "Will you play for me sometime? I'd love to hear you play."

She pulls back, surprise on her face. "You want to hear me play?"

"Why wouldn't I?"

"I would love to. Of course, I'll have to find another

violin." Hurt laces her tone. I know she's still upset about her violin.

I point to the life-size violin in front of me, covered in flowers. "Think you can play on this? I can probably get them to let me take it home."

Her laughter ringing out is music to my ears. "Yes, I'm sure this would make the same sounds as I'm used to." She's grinning as she pulls away from me, dancing through the flowers. Bloody hell, how can I be in so deep with someone so fast?

"Maybe I could even play the piano for you." Zara's eyes are twinkling. She's glowing with the sun reflecting off her. She looks happier than I've seen her this last week. Instead of fear underlying her every mood, she's alight with happiness. I know she didn't want to be thrust into this position, but right now, I'm glad it was her.

"You're looking awfully thoughtful there, Your Highness."

"Just thinking about how good you look there." The blush that creeps over her skin stirs something inside me. Women fall at my feet, but it's been a while since one has appeared indifferent. And that's exactly how Zara was acting towards me. But after our event the other night, I'm seeing a new side to her. And damn, I can't help but be drawn to her.

"Excuse me, Your Highness. Lady Zara." Olivia is back at my side. "Are you ready to move on to the next exhibit?" Zara tucks a loose strand of hair behind her ear, coming to stand by my side.

"This was beautiful." Her eyes are still roaming over the instruments. Running my hand down Zara's arm, a shock of electricity hits me.

Shite, that's new. Zara's eyes swing to mine, and her eyes look so brown they're black. Did she feel that too?

"Are you ready?" Olivia's voice brings me back to the present.

"Yes, let's go." Zara breaks the staredown we're having. The soft sway of her hips as she walks away from me has my dick stirring in my pants. This is bad. This is very, very bad.

Chapter Ten

ZARA

"**S**o was the Royal Flower Show everything you'd hoped it would be?" James's presence is a calming weight behind me. It had been an interesting afternoon with him. I've felt the growing desire with him this past week, but today, it was like he felt it too.

"It was brilliant." Pushing open the black door to my house, James lingers in the doorway. "Would you like to come in for dinner?" I ask suddenly. A few flashbulbs are popping across the street. James's smile is bright as he follows me inside.

"Are we ordering takeaway?" He toes off his shoes as I kick off my wedges. James follows me into the kitchen. It feels intimate, him in his bare feet padding across my house. Never in a million years did I think I'd have the future King in my house.

"If you're okay waiting, I can whip something up."

He's rolling up the sleeves of his shirt. The fine dusting of dark hair on his arms is drool worthy. James is at ease here, helping himself to a drink.

"I'm happy waiting. Can I be your sous-chef?" He's

swirling the drink, leaning against the counter. He looks so at home. I like having him here with me.

"Make me a gin and tonic, and then you can help."

"You've got this bossing people around thing down. You're fit to be Queen," he chuckles, winking at me.

"Well, I guess it's a good thing I'm marrying a prince."

He winces at that comment, as I get everything out of the fridge. Maybe he's a bit more sensitive to this arranged marriage than I thought.

"Is salmon okay?"

"Perfect." He hands me my drink, our fingers brushing. Lingering. I'm not supposed to fall for this man. It makes it that much harder to hold on to my anger towards my father if whatever this is between James and me is real. He has a kingdom to lead. I have students to teach. There's no way this can be real.

I take a large sip of my drink, needing to cool off.

"Alright, what do I get to do?" James claps his hands, rubbing them together.

I place a bag of carrots and a knife in front of him. "You're making the veggies. Just need to peel them and cut them."

"Peel and cut. Can't be too hard, can it?" He gives me a smirk, before opening the carrots. The salmon's already prepared, so I turn the knobs to start the oven, but my focus is on James.

The delicate way his fingers move the knife is hypnotizing. He's butchering the carrots, but he's doing it with such pride, I can't stop him.

"What?" He holds his hands out, like he can't understand why I'm staring at him.

Laughter bubbles out of me. "It's just, you're not doing it properly. You need to peel them, then cut."

He looks down at the mess he's made. "Shite. I'm not doing a very good job impressing you, am I?"

"That would mean I want to be impressed." I hip check him, moving in beside him.

"Ouch. You sure do know how to make a man feel special."

"Here, let me show you." I grab his hand with mine, the carrot with the other. My hands are dainty compared to his. I slowly move my hand, guiding his movements. Heat is radiating off him.

"I'm not a very good sous-chef if you're doing most of the work." His breath is hot on my cheek.

"Everyone has to learn somehow." Tilting my chin upward, his lips are right there. It would be so easy to lean up and capture his lips. To feel the stubble under my fingers as I take what I want.

"Zara." James's free hand wraps around my neck, his thumb on my pulse. No doubt he can feel the rapid beat. The heat of his hand settles in my core. Butterflies are dancing in my belly as he moves closer, his lips only an inch away from mine.

The ding of the oven breaks through the fog of lust clouding my brain. "Guess you better get that in the oven." James pulls away. I lament the loss of him.

I set the salmon on a pan, putting it in the oven before helping James finish the carrots. The tension from earlier is gone. It's for the best, right? Falling for this man is a bad idea.

"Put the carrots in the pan, and then I'll top off our drinks. Shouldn't take long for them to cook," I instruct.

"Look at me. Making dinner like a pro."

I can't help the laugh that bubbles out of me. "I'll give you an A for effort."

"Guess I'll stick to leading the country, eh?"

I shrug my shoulders. "How about another A for effort?"

"Is this what I have to look forward to for the next fifty years? Cheeky little bugger, you are." The smile plastered on James's face matches my own. I like this side of him. He never shows it to the press, but I like that I get to see it. It goes beyond the charming façade. He's fun, but also has a vulnerable side.

James and I continue our easy conversation while dinner cooks. I didn't think it would be like this. I thought it would be hard to be around the future King. But it's anything but. It's easy and carefree.

The buzzer sounds, pulling me away from the man holding my attention. "Grab some plates and we'll be ready to eat." I point in the direction of the correct cabinet, and he grabs what we need.

Plating dinner, we move to my small table that overlooks the back courtyard.

"Cheers." James clinks his glass against mine, extending his long legs across the small space.

"Cheers."

My eyes are drawn to him as he takes a bite, years of royal protocol obvious in the way he eats. "Zara, love. This is delicious. Better than any Michelin-starred meal that I've had." He dives right back in, taking another hearty bite.

"You flatter me. It's not that good."

"I'll be the judge of that." The wink causes those butterflies to stir again. This is why he's the "playboy prince." This charm he has always makes everyone fall at his feet. I hate that I'm one of them.

"So, how are you doing with everything?" I ask, digging into my own meal.

"Everything?" He looks up, midchew.

"With the whole reason why we're here. With you now

first in line for the throne." He puts down his fork, giving me a pensive stare, his brow furrowing slightly.

"At first, I wanted to be mad at Ellie. But then I could see how miserable she was, and I couldn't really blame her." He swirls his drink before taking a sip. "And now, the pressure is on. I can no longer run around and ignore the duties of what I was born to do."

James's shoulders are tense as he leans over the table.

"The press is no longer eating out of the palm of your hand?"

He grins as he goes back to eating. "No, I wish. They were much easier to please when I could just flash a smile and continue on my way. Now, I actually have to do more than just shake hands."

"Have you given any more thought to which charities are going to be your new patronages?"

"They've already been hand-selected for me, so just a matter of deciding. Not that I'll get much choice there either."

"And you really won't get a say in what you want to do?"

James's deep blue eyes stare into mine. It's so easy to get lost in them. "They are handpicked by the Queen."

Ahh. "So not things you're really interested in." James is very easy to read. He is not happy about this.

"Charities have been dropped in my lap since I was old enough to be a patron. But I want to find something I'm passionate about. I don't want to just go through the motions."

"And what are you passionate about?" I push my empty plate out of the way, resting my chin in my hand.

"What are *you* passionate about?" He gives me that smile that is known to drop panties of women everywhere.

I hate that I feel it all over. That liquid fire spreads through my body at the sight of it.

"I'm not the one that needs to get my life together, James. I believe that's you."

"Why can't I just use your passion? You love music?" I give him a small nod. "I'll go with music then."

"You can't just take my passion, James," I say on a laugh.

"Damn. And here I thought it was going to be that easy."

I stand, grabbing our plates and taking them to the sink. "Maybe I can help you narrow down the list."

"You don't have to do that." James is behind me, refilling his drink.

"If we're going to be married, I might as well be a sounding board for you."

"What a good fiancée you are." I can't quell the butterflies that start fluttering in my stomach again. I hate how he affects me like this.

"You have to keep me around for a reason. Now, start talking."

James finishes refilling his drink before hopping onto the counter. "So bossy." He takes a hearty sip of his drink before he does what he's told. "Maybe I could just make Sean's art school my charity."

"Would your sister like that?" I give him a stern eye.

"No, probably not." He's staring into his drink, the weight of the world heavy on his shoulders. "Do we really have to do this?"

I walk over to where he is, resisting the urge to put my hands on his strong thighs. "James. I'm not trying to make this into a big thing. Maybe just start thinking about it. You might find that if you do, some inspiration might strike you. Remember what I said? Start small. You're not becoming King tomorrow."

James pulls me between his legs, his fingers dancing up and down my arm. Goose pimples break out in their path. "You'll make a very good Queen, you know that?"

A shy smile breaks out across my face. "What makes you say that?"

"You see past my bullshit and put me in my place. Not to mention, you had Olivia wrapped around your finger. She loved you."

Laughter escapes my lips. "I passed my Queen lessons then?"

"With flying colours." James's eyes keep drifting to my lips. Heat is radiating off him, pulling me into his orbit. His gaze is soft as he leans forward, ever so slowly, and captures my lips with his.

My mind goes blank. My body leans into his, wanting to bottle the electricity shooting through me.

All thought leaves my mind as James's lips meet mine. They're warm and soft and taste like scotch. Butterflies are swarming in my stomach as I lean into the kiss and James pulls me closer into him. Big, warm hands are a hot brand on my body. Everywhere they touch, I'm singed with a deep desire for more contact.

I've never had such a visceral reaction to a kiss. Fire is sweeping through my body. A moan escapes, causing James to sweep his tongue into my mouth. My hands fist in his shirt, tugging him closer to me, deepening the kiss.

Keeping him close to me with one hand, I thread my fingers through the waves at the nape of his neck. The strands are like silk under my fingers, as I twist my hand through the curls. A deep groan reverberates through him.

James is off the counter and backing me into the wall.

His lips blaze a hot trail down my neck as he grinds his erection into me. I'm shameless in my need to get closer to him as I rock my hips into him. Desire snakes down my spine to my core. An ache so deep settles within me. I want more. More of his touch. More of his lips on mine. More of James.

"Fuck, Z." James pulls back, his breath hot on my cheek. Squeezing my eyes shut, I try to tamp down the need inside me. James's fingers brush over my neck, up to my jaw before tracing my lips. Fireworks are exploding inside my body at the slightest touch.

I skate my hands around his waist, not wanting to lose his touch. His strong muscles flex under my fingertips. "As much as I would love to continue this tonight, I've got a packed schedule tomorrow, and you have school."

"But you do plan on continuing this?" Hunger laces my husky voice. I want more.

James takes another kiss. Another deep, soul-stirring kiss. Say what you will about him being a playboy, but he knows how to kiss a woman.

"Does that answer your question?"

Chapter Eleven

JAMES

I've never been brought to my knees like that. Bloody hell, I've been distracted all day. That kiss last night rocked me to my core. Zara has wormed her way under my skin, and I have no idea what to do about it. It's unsettling, this feeling of wanting more with a woman. Women can always count on me for a good time. A quick romp before said woman signs an NDA and is on her way.

But with Zara? I want more.

"Your Highness?" Shite, I've been spacing off again. "Would you like to visit the new children's wing of the hospital?"

I give the hospital director my winningest smile. "Absolutely."

She walks me back, giving me a rundown of the new ward, sponsored in part by one of the royal patronages. "And what are all of these children in the hospital for?"

As we enter the area, I'm assaulted with bright colours and happy voices. The walls are painted with murals of the jungle and ocean, and the waiting area has books and toys of all kinds strewn about.

"These children are short term patients. Broken bones, minor surgeries. We have a play area for families while they're waiting," she says, gesturing to the area behind me, "and the nurses' station is set up in the middle, so they can keep an eye on all the children."

"This is a wonderful setup you have here." It's nice to see good work being done with the royal patronages.

"Are you really the prince?" A small boy in a wheelchair stops in front of me. A large cast overtakes one of his legs.

"Do you think I am?" I squat down so I'm on his level.

"I thought princes wore crowns." He gives me a puzzled look.

"No, stupid. Only princesses wear crowns!" A girl appears at his side, looking remarkably like him.

"I'm not stupid!" the boy cries. Oh dear, what have I gotten myself into here?

"Victoria. George. That's enough." A haggard looking woman runs up behind them. "I'm so sorry, Your Highness." She dips into a low curtsy. "We've been cooped up in the hospital a few days longer than we'd like."

"It's quite alright. What brings you in here?"

"Obviously it's him." The little girl rolls her eyes at me, before wandering back to the play area. Her mother looks like she wants the ground to swallow her whole. Ouch. Guess I don't have a fan.

"I'm so sorry about my daughter. She's ready to head home." She gives me a soft look.

"I can't imagine being cooped up in here. I bet you're ready to get home. And how'd you break your leg, George?" I'm down on his level again.

"I broke my leg playing football."

"And who's your favourite football team?"

"Chelsea. They're the best! My room is blue to match the team!" He's so excited about his football team.

"Chelsea just happens to be my favourite too, but don't tell anyone. Maybe I can get you some tickets once you're healed up."

His eyes widen in delight. "I've never been to a match before!"

I nod at Charles behind me, indicating for him to make it happen. "Well, you get better, and then you'll be able to go."

"You're the best prince we have!" He gives me a high five as the mother bows and heaps praise on me.

The director is beaming at me as we finish our tour. "You were quite the hit today, Your Highness."

"It's always a pleasure to visit here. Thank you for all you do." I shake her hand as the car is brought around.

"Thank you. It's been wonderful to have you here." She bows as I make my way into the car.

"That was quite the showing you had, James." Charles climbs in behind me as we speed off towards the palace. "The press was eating it up."

"I wasn't doing it for them." Although, it's an added benefit that the press was here today. Between Charles and my mum, I'm being told to watch every move right now, as I can't take any more bad press.

"Either way, it was a good day. We'll get that family set up with a day they'll never forget with Chelsea. Nothing like a special outing from the prince."

A special outing. There's someone else who could do with a special outing.

"Charles. Any chance you could make a special outing happen tonight?"

"Sir?"

Giving him my idea, he immediately goes to work as I

pull up my phone and dial the number to the one woman whom I can't seem to resist.

"Hi, James." Her voice is smooth as she picks up on the first ring. I love that there is no pretence in letting me wait.

"Zara, love. Any chance you're free tonight?" I look over at Charles, and he's nodding to me. Being the prince, I can make things happen. "Say, seven?"

"What do you have planned?" I love the playfulness in her voice.

"Is you saying yes contingent on what the plans are?"

"I don't know. I might have a hot date tonight already."

A hot spike of jealousy rages through me. "A hot date?"

"Yes. He's quite old, actually. Ancient, really. Known for composing a number of symphonies."

I huff out a sigh. "Way to give a man a heart attack. Is it Beethoven or Mozart tonight?"

Her laughter on the other end of the line is soothing. Since when does a woman's laugh settle me? "It was going to be Mozart. But I suppose he'll still be around tomorrow."

"Perfect. I'll pick you up at seven. Wear something fancy."

"Fancy? Where are you taking me, James?"

"You'll just have to wait and see."

"ZARA, YOU LOOK ABSOLUTELY STUNNING." The long red dress with flowers decorating it hugs her lithe frame. Her long brown waves curl past her shoulders. She's breathtaking.

"You don't look so bad yourself." She smooths her

hands over the lapels of my tux. I waste no time capturing those plump lips of hers. She opens to me immediately. The softness of her tongue is a match striking the fire within me. I don't know how I'll ever get enough of this woman. If I didn't have this special night planned, I'd toss her over my shoulder and take her upstairs right this second.

"As much as I would love to stay here with you all night," she whispers, pulling back, "I do want to see what this surprise is that has us dressed to the nines."

"Well then,"—I tuck a strand of hair behind her ear— "let's get going, shall we?"

I give her my arm as I lead us outside. Flashes are bright in the spring evening. Zara stiffens at my side but doesn't waver. We ignore the questions shouted at us as we approach the waiting car.

"A limo? Where are you taking me tonight?" The door is opened and she slides into the limo. A bottle of champagne is chilling in the ice bucket.

"I promise you, you'll like it." I pop the cork and hand her a glass as the limo pulls away from the curb. "To surprises." I clink my glass against hers and take a sip.

Zara gulps half of hers down before turning her eyes on me. "You might just be the biggest surprise of all, James." Her eyes are dark as she takes my hand in hers. Her delicate fingers trace the veins on the back of my hand. It's intoxicating. What this woman does to me is unlike anything I've ever felt.

"And why is that?"

"Because I expected the Playboy Prince, and instead, I got Prince Charming."

"Maybe I'm a little of both." I turn my hand in hers, linking our hands together.

"You've got more charm in your pinkie finger than

most people could ever hope to have." She turns a radiant smile on me, one that hits me directly in the centre of my chest. Fecking hell. I really am falling for this woman, aren't I?

"Your Highness. We've arrived."

Zara's gaze is pulled from mine as we come to the side door of the building. "You don't plan on killing me, do you?"

"Now why would I make you dress up if I was planning to off you?" I chuckle as I take her hand.

"Stranger things have happened, I'm sure." The door opens, and we're led through a long hall before we enter the lobby. Red velvet lines the wall, and two grand staircases circle their way upstairs. A crystal chandelier reflects soft light throughout the room.

"James. What are we doing here at the symphony?" The pressure on my arm causes me to stop.

"You are a music fan, aren't you?"

"Yes, but why are we the only people here?" Her voice is quiet as she surveys the empty room.

"There are some perks of being a prince." I pull her forward as her mouth drops open in awe. The doors to the concert hall open, and we're led to the best seats in the house. A bottle of champagne and a tray of chocolate-covered strawberries await us. Just like I planned.

Zara is glued to her spot, standing and staring at the stage as the orchestra starts to make their way to their seats. Her eyes are glassy as she glances around the empty room, before turning to face me.

"You rented out the orchestra for me?"

I can only shrug. "Well, technically I paid for an extra performance tonight. They only perform on the weekends, so this is our own personal show." I spin her around and rest my hands on her slim waist. "I want to experience this with you." I drop a kiss on her exposed neck. "I want to experience what you feel when you listen to music."

"James." Her voice catches in her throat, stopping me in my tracks. "This is one of the most thoughtful things anyone has ever done for me."

The look on her face hits me square in the chest. Pure happiness radiates from her. I would buy the entire orchestra and have them perform for her every night if it meant I could keep this look on her face.

"Your Highness." The attendant hands us each a glass of champagne as noise from the stage has Zara moving to her seat. I'm helpless to follow. A tune I'm not familiar with has Zara clutching my arm. "I don't think I've ever heard the music this loud in here."

The sheer awe on her face is striking. I've never seen someone so passionate about anything before. She's in a trance as the music continues to rise and lower around us.

As a new piece starts, Zara gasps, turning to look at me. "This is my favourite piece. It's so beautiful and so romantic."

"And why is it so romantic?" I lean in, whispering in her ear.

"It's the dance of two lovers. It's the will they, won't they. It's the excitement of a new relationship when you find one another. It crescendos with them finally acting on their love for one another."

Bloody hell, I've never been a big fan of classical music, but this might be my new favourite piece. The passion in Zara's eyes as she describes her love of this piece is unmatched. It's not hard to feel her love of music when she describes it like a real-life, breathing thing.

"Have you ever felt something like this before?" I ask, as she turns to me, her eyes sparkling in the dark auditorium.

"Not before, no." Zara sips her champagne, before taking a small bite of a strawberry. Before she sets it down, I grab her wrist and finish it off. Her eyes are hungry as she licks her lips.

"And now?" I drop a kiss on the inside of her delicate wrist.

"Now it's as if I'm living this song."

I don't waste another minute. I pull Zara to me and she's as needy as I am. The music peaks around us as we ignite. I can't remember the last time a kiss has ever felt so good. The need. The passion.

We're moving in sync with the beat of the music. The space between us is too much. Thank God we're the only people here, because I pull Zara into my lap.

"Oh God, James." Her voice is a whisper as I suck and nibble on her neck. Her throaty moans do something to me. I feel it down to my bones. The ache in my groin needs a release that only she can give me.

"Zara, love," I purr, tugging her earlobe. "I have to have you tonight. I can't wait any longer."

Zara pulls back, lust clouding her beautiful eyes.

"I want nothing more." Her fingers trail down my neck, leaving a trail of fire in their wake. Shite, I don't want to waste another minute here, but I want to give her a night she'll remember. "But we have to stay until the end. This piece really is my favourite."

She gives me a happy smile as she curls up into my side. Zara is humming along, the vibrations against my neck going straight to my dick. I've spent many a night wrapped around different women. It was always the perfect no-strings-attached situation. It wasn't easy having Mum shove this whole idea of an arranged marriage at me.

But right now? Nothing beats this. Sitting with Zara in

my lap, doing the thing she loves most in the world. What I wouldn't give to spend all my nights like this.

I want this woman. I want her with every ounce of my being. To make her mine in every sense of the word. And tonight? Tonight, Zara will be mine.

Chapter Twelve

It's been a magical night. One of the best in my life, in fact. No one has ever done anything like this for me before. Most men I've dated don't understand my love of music, something that I cherish because my mum loved music the same way. It's the way I carry her with me. It's a part of my soul.

But James understands. He planned the perfect evening for just the two of us. Away from the prying eyes of the paparazzi.

"Are you ready to go?" James's voice is quiet as the music stops. It's dark as the lights on the stage dim. Tears prick the back of my eyes as I let this moment wash over me. I'm not ready to leave. I want to stay here in this empty auditorium, with James in my arms.

"Z? Are you still with me?"

I love when he calls me that. I pull back, staring into his dark eyes. Butterflies erupt in my stomach. His eyes are searching mine. I lean in, taking a kiss. His hands roam over my back, hot skin on skin. I cup his face, deepening the kiss. I know it's not good form to be sitting here like this, but I don't care. A need like I've never known is coursing through my veins. I need James.

"Your Highness." James's security officers break the moment. His eyes are heavy and his lips swollen. I love that I bring this out in him. "The car is ready if you are."

"Thank you. We'll be right there." He doesn't break eye contact. He starts to stand, forcing me off his lap. Before he starts to make his way out, I grab him and pull him back.

"James." My voice is raspy with lust. My eyes are on the departing orchestra. "Thank you. I will never forget this night."

The smile he gives me causes my heart to flutter. He really is the sexiest man I've ever met. And not just because of that smile. There's so much more underneath all that sex appeal that he doesn't let the world see.

"You're worth it, Zara. Don't you ever forget that." His breath ghosts my lips as he holds me close to him. "Now, are you ready to continue our evening elsewhere?" His eyes hold a knowing glint.

"My place then?"

His lips barely make contact with mine. "Your place. Let's go." James turns and pulls me along behind him, the same way we came in. The limo is at the door, ready to whisk us off. Sliding in, James wastes no time pulling me across him again. This time, his hands find their way up my dress.

"I've been dreaming of this."

His lips make their way down my neck, nibbling and sucking as they go.

"Oh God," I groan. His lips cause heat to gather in my core.

"You drive me wild, Zara." James pulls back, staring into my eyes.

Lust. Passion. Desire. It's all reflected in his eyes. I move closer to him, needing his lips on mine. His hands move to my arse, grinding me over his hard length. It feels amazing.

"See how you make me feel?" he whispers. I drop my forehead to his, rocking into him. "I bet if I slipped my finger inside you, you'd be wet."

I bite down on my lip to keep the needy moans inside as his finger trails over my hot core. There's no hiding my desire for him.

"Fuck, Z. Have you been like this all night?"

I trail kisses along his jaw back to his ear, tugging it between my teeth. I can feel him get harder underneath me. "Yes. When a man does something like you did for a woman, it's a huge turn-on."

"Duly noted, love." James turns, tugging my bottom lip between his teeth. A shot of lust moves through me as the car comes to a stop.

"We've arrived, sir." The driver's voice crackles through the small space.

"Still okay if I come inside?" James trails his fingers lightly over my cheeks.

"I might combust if you don't."

"I can't stay the night. It's bad form if they see me leave in the morning, but Christ, Zara. I need to be with you tonight."

"Then what are we waiting for?" I slide off him, moving to the door as it opens. I add a little sway to my hips as we make our way inside the house.

I barely have the door unlocked and open when James is at my back. As soon as he kicks the door closed, his lips brush my neck with hot, wet kisses and then move down my back. Thank God for the open back on this dress.

James's hands slide under the material at my hips as I throw my head back, guiding us to my room.

"James. If you don't stop, we'll be doing this in the entryway." I spin in his arms.

"I'm not seeing the problem." His eyes are playful as they rake over me.

"Bedroom. Now." I walk backwards, keeping my eyes on him as he loosens his tie. I can't wait to feel those hands all over my bare skin. Inside me. Driving me towards pleasure.

Sweeping my skirt in one hand, I race up the stairs, James hot on my trail. His hands grab me as I push open my door.

"I can't wait to get you out of this dress." James's voice burns with need. I tug the zipper down as he stalks towards me, like a cheetah on the hunt for his prey.

He holds the material at my shoulders, before sliding it down. The heavy material falls down around me, leaving me in only my thong and heels.

"Fecking hell. You are beautiful." His voice is dripping with need as his hands light an inferno inside me.

His thumbs skate over my nipples, turning them into diamonds. I arch into his touch.

"You're wearing far too many clothes." I fist my hands in his shirt, wanting to feel his muscles under my fingers.

My knees hit the bed and I fall back, my body aching with need as I watch him. James starts unbuttoning his shirt, painstakingly slow. Finally throwing off his shirt, his abs are on full display. A smattering of hair coats his chest, and a dark trail of hair disappears below his pants.

I try to quell the ache coiling in my centre, but James grabs my legs, throwing them apart.

"Your pleasure is mine tonight." Pulling me to the edge of the bed, he sinks to his knees. James plants searing kisses as he moves up my leg, getting closer to where I really want him. "I've dreamed about this pussy." His finger ghosting over the sheer fabric is enough to make me come.

"Damn it, James! I need your mouth—" I'm cut off as he finally sweeps his tongue over my slit. Ripping the tiny shred of fabric off me, he sucks my clit into his mouth. He moves his tongue with expert precision as he sinks two fingers inside me. My heels dig deep into his back, wanting to keep him where he is.

I'm riding his tongue and fingers without shame. I've never felt so wanton, so sexy, as I do with this skilled man who is driving me closer and closer to orgasm.

"You taste like a dream, Zara. I can't wait until you explode on my tongue," he whispers to me between licking and sucking. A few more strokes and I'm coming undone. Stars explode around me as the most intense orgasm sweeps through me. The only thing keeping me grounded is James's hand on my stomach. I'm a writhing mess beneath him.

James pulls off me slowly, his lips glistening with my release. I pull him over me, his weight settling on top of me, and claim his lips with mine.

It's hard.

It's raw.

It's sinful.

It's everything.

My hands are shaky from my orgasm as I undo his belt buckle. Reaching into his boxers, I pull his hard cock out. He's big, but not overwhelming. Velvet steel in my hand.

"Fuuuck, Zara." James's voice is drawn tight as I work my hand over his shaft, a bead of precum leaking from the tip. He's rocking into my hand as I move faster. James grabs my hand, pulling it out.

"If you keep doing that, I'm going to blow in your

hand. What would that say about me?" He rocks back, his hands holding my arms above my head.

"That I turn you on?"

"That you do." He sucks the tight bud of my nipple into his mouth.

"The feeling is mutual." My voice is breathy as he moves to my other breast, lavishing it with attention. It's a line of fire straight to my pulsing core, driving me closer and closer to another orgasm.

"If you don't get inside me right now, I'm going to combust."

James pops off me with a grin and stands. "We can't have that, now, can we?" He grabs his wallet as he kicks off his pants. Fully naked now, he is a fine specimen of a man. Abs for days, powerful lines, and that cock. Lord, am I ready to have it inside me.

"You're drooling."

Pushing up on my elbows, I scoot back on the bed. "Can you blame me when you look like that?" I wave my hand in his direction as he rolls a condom down his thick cock.

"You apparently don't know how sexy you look lying there in your heels. I want to do very dirty, very bad things to you, Zara."

"Then please come do very bad things to me." I spread my legs, touching my already sensitive clit. His eyes narrow in on where I'm rubbing myself. I'm slick with need as James strokes himself.

"This is the hottest thing I've ever seen, Zara." He crawls over me, settling back on top of me.

"It might get hotter." Looping my legs around him, I flip us over. There's a hunger in James's eyes unlike anything I've ever seen. Sliding my slick pussy up and down his hard shaft, I draw closer and closer to another orgasm. Right before I tip over the edge, I sink down on top of him.

"James. Oh God, James!" It's good. So good. Better than anything I've ever experienced in my life. The stretch of him filling me gives way to pure pleasure. It takes everything I have not to come immediately.

Clutching his hard pecs, I start moving, rocking my hips over him. Lifting up and sinking back down. "Yes, Zara. Keep going." James's hands move up my sides, cupping my breasts in his hands. Kneading, tweaking my nipples to the point of pain.

Drawing my nails down his chest, I play with myself again. James must like it if his quickening thrusts are anything to go by.

"You need to come now, Zara. Bloody hell, take it." He thrusts harder as his hands are bruising on my hips.

Another thrust and I'm crashing over the edge. I'm boneless as I fall on top of James. Electricity shoots through me at the strength of my orgasm. He holds me to him as he comes, pulsing deep inside me.

"Holy shit." My voice is muffled as my face is buried in James's neck. His spicy smell mixed with the heavy scent of sex is potent. I can't remember the last time I've come so hard. Twice.

But I also can't remember the last time I've ever felt so safe and secure in someone's arms. Never in a million years did I think it would happen with the prince.

"I wish I didn't have to leave tonight. I want to stay here with you all night." His fingers trail a path down my back. I love his need to touch me.

"If only the press wouldn't track our every move. There's nothing I want more than to wake up with you beside me."

"I'm glad you don't want to kick me out the first chance you get."

I push off him, staring into his eyes, and I see the insecurity lingering there. "Why in the world would you think that?" I brush my hands over his chest, the smattering of hair coarse under my fingertips.

"It's what usually happens when I'm with a woman. Once they get their fill of the 'playboy prince,' I'm useless."

"Well, now I might kick you out. Do you know nothing about women?" Incredulity laces my voice as I smack his chest.

"Sorry. Not to bring it up, but I just don't want to leave. There's nothing I want more than to stay here with you tonight. I've never had that feeling before."

My eyes soften, raking over his handsome face. "It's not just you. I hate that they're probably out there wondering what we're doing in here. I just want to stay wrapped up in you."

I hate that he can't stay. I hate that the paparazzi are sitting outside my house, waiting for a picture of him leaving at an indecent hour.

I nuzzle back into him, kissing his neck. His scruff is scratchy against my lips. "I wish our every move wasn't watched."

"I promise, it won't always be like this. We're new. A hot commodity."

"I find that hard to believe." I sit up, pulling off him. I lament the loss of him immediately.

James flips us around, throwing his leg over me. "Zara. I promise, I won't let anything happen to you."

"You can't make that promise." My fingers move on their own, tracing over the beautiful features of his face.

"Well, hopefully they'll back off. In case you haven't heard, they are eating up my recent appearances."

"They'll be forgetting all about the playboy, and only want this prince I get."

He looks down between us. "Well, maybe not *this* prince. This would certainly undo all the good work I've been doing."

I give him a playful smile. My hands glide down his chest, his cock already hardening at my touch. "Well then, if we're going to undo all that good work, might as well get our money's worth."

Chapter Thirteen

ZARA

"You little minx." Marnie's voice startles me from the quiet of my classroom. I've taken to eating lunch in my classroom to avoid the stares and whispers from other teachers. It feels like I'm back in secondary school and I'm left outside the clique.

"What on earth are you talking about?" I pierce her with a look. I have no idea what she's referring to.

"The photos of James leaving your house last night. I want all of the juicy details." She plops herself down in a chair next to my desk, her eyes dancing with intrigue.

"The paparazzi will be the end of me. Why is everyone so interested in me? I'm a nobody." I look down at my lunch, no longer hungry.

"Honey." Marnie's hand is warm on my forearm, pulling my eyes up to meet hers. "You are no longer a nobody. You are dating the first in line to the British throne. Of course they are going to be interested in you."

"I just wish that we could date like two normal people. Stay over at one another's houses and not have to worry about appearances if he sneaks out in the middle of the night."

Marnie's smile turns positively gleeful. "And just why would he be sneaking out in the middle of the night?"

My smile mirrors hers as I glance around the room, ensuring we're alone. "Because we slept together," I whisper.

"Tell me everything!" Marnie shouts, clapping her hands. "I want all the details. How was he? Does his dick live up to all the hype?"

"Shh. We're still in school!" I wave her down, trying to keep her quiet, but it's no use. "Of course it was amazing. I don't think it's ever been so good."

"I can tell by the way you're blushing." She wags her finger over my face. "You're like a schoolgirl who got kissed by the cute boy for the first time."

"I can't help it. He was so good. Amazing. Fantastic." I hated that James had to leave. Even the few hours we spent together last night weren't enough. I want more than just these stolen moments together.

"Best shag of your life?"

I nod.

"I knew it. There's no way he'd get into that many panties if he didn't know how to use what God gave him."

"He is more than just what's in his pants." I hate that even my closest friend only sees what the press puts out there. There's so much more to James than just his colourful past with women.

James's presence in my life has rocked me to the core. When we were told this arranged marriage would need to work, my walls went up. How did anyone expect me to fall in love with the "playboy prince"? The one who was more concerned with the women he slept with than the work he did? But now, I'm seeing a different side to James than the one that's splashed all across the media. He wants to do good work. He wants the respect of his citizens.

And now, he's slipped his way past my carefully constructed walls.

"I'll have to meet him then. Just because he has you falling in lust with him, doesn't mean he'll pass the best friend test." It's possible I'm falling more than just in lust with him, but she doesn't need to know that. Not yet anyway.

"How about Friday? There's no palace-approved event, so I could convince him to come over."

"Can't we go to the palace? I've never been before." Marnie gives me her best sad face to try and convince me.

"You know he doesn't actually live at Buckingham, right?"

"Fine. Kensington. I guess I'll have to rough it." She rolls her eyes at me. "I've already been to your house countless times. Why would we go there?"

"James likes coming over to my place."

"Oh, and why is that?" She waggles her eyebrows at me.

"Stop it, Marnie. Not everything has to do with sex."

"But with that man, it should."

I stand, pulling her up with me. "Marnie, I love you, but time to go. I need to finish my lunch before the students come back."

"Spoilsport." She sticks her tongue out at me as she waltzes out the door. Is this what my life is going to come to? Every person I know asking about the prince? Dad has remained relatively quiet on that front. Probably because he knows how angry I was at first. It's the twenty-first century. Arranged marriages aren't common here. But now? The thought isn't nearly as unsettling as it once was.

"I CAN'T BELIEVE I'm meeting the prince!" Marnie's voice is a loud squeal in my ear.

"You have to calm down. He's just a regular person." The car is pulling up to the palace gates, and my nerves are starting to get the better of me. Marnie is one of the most important people in my life. What if she doesn't like James? What if she only sees his past and not the person he's becoming with me? Shite, I'm a lot deeper into this relationship than I thought.

"He's going to rule the country, Zara. Of course I'm going to freak out." We pull up outside his door in the courtyard and Marnie flies out the door, not even bothering to wait for the driver to open it. James is standing there, casual as ever in jeans and a dress shirt, laughing as Marnie curtsies to him. She's going to ruin this for me before it ever gets started.

"I'm so sorry about her," I whisper, taking James's hand, who is now helping me out of the car. Ever the gentleman.

"Not the first time that's happened." He gives me a wink that has butterflies swarming my stomach. No wonder women fall at his feet. "Now, since this is Zara's first time here, would you both like a tour?"

"Not necessary."

"Absolutely." Marnie and I answer at the same time, and I give her a hard look.

"What? This will be your home soon, might as well learn the ropes." She winks at me as James takes my hand.

"She has a point, you know."

"Okay, Prince Charming. Lead the way." I sweep my

hand in front of me, as James gives me a soft stare. Those butterflies in my stomach? They're ready to take flight.

James gives us a tour of the main part of the apartment. Twenty rooms spread over several floors would be too much tonight. To be honest, it's a little overwhelming the deeper into the apartment we get. He's leading us around one of the upstairs rooms, but I can't focus on it.

I've always loved the quiet of my little house, tucked away in a nice London neighbourhood. But seeing where James lives reiterates the fast-approaching future and what my life is going to be.

"Hey, Marnie, why don't you wait for us in the living room. My friend Oliver should be here soon."

"Fab." She waggles her fingers in our direction, as James nods to one of his advisors who is close by and shows Marnie out of the hall we're in.

"What's on your mind, love?" James is leaning against the window, haloed by the setting sun over the palace gardens.

"This is all just a bit overwhelming."

"What's overwhelming? A twenty-room 'apartment' on palace grounds that will soon be your home before eventually moving into another palace? Being trailed everywhere by security, for every minute of every day?"

"When you put it like that…" I trail off. Ornate gilding lines the high ceilings. Velvet lines every wall here. Nothing about this place is simple. And soon, it's going to be the everyday reality of my life.

A worried look washes over James's face. It's rare that he's anything but happy, which is something I'm finding so hard to comprehend when faced with the press now on a daily basis.

"What are you worried about?" His warm hand envelops mine, pulling me between his legs.

My free hand plays with the buttons on his shirt. "I'm a schoolteacher, James. How am I supposed to come to terms with this life?"

James tilts my chin up to face him. His brow is furrowed as pain pools in his blue eyes. "It's a learning process, love. No one expects you to know everything on day one."

"But what if I call a foreign dignitary the wrong title? Or trip and flash everyone?"

"I called the King of Sweden the Prince of Sweden if it makes you feel better. And have you seen the paparazzi's coverage of me?"

"Way to quell my worries by bringing up your dick hanging out for all the world to see."

"Sorry, bad example."

His big hands wrap around my back, pulling me into his chest, tucking my head under his chin. "Did you really call the King of Sweden the Prince?"

Laughter vibrates through him. "In my defense, he looked really young. I mean, what seventy-year-old man doesn't have grey hair?"

"That's your basis for insulting the king of another country?"

"I know this might surprise you, but I'm not perfect."

A smile plays on my lips. "Hate to burst your bubble, but the mere fact that I'm here confirms that statement."

"Ouch." He pinches my side. "Gloves are coming off now."

Standing here in James's arms is settling. His presence soothes me in a way that once set my teeth on edge. "So, is this what our life will be like? Each of us having our own charities and events? Coming home to this big apartment together by ourselves?"

"You know we'll be moving into Clarence House soon after we're married, right?"

A sigh escapes my lips. "One more thing to adjust to."

James drops his forehead to mine. "I've seen you these last few weeks. After a few minor mishaps, you've adapted well. You have people eating out of the palm of your hand. Besides, I think it sounds pretty nice."

"What, eating out of my hand?"

"No, you loon. Coming home to you every night."

If I saw butterflies flying out of me right now, I wouldn't be surprised. James continues to shock me. When we were first told that we were to be wed, I thought it would be a loveless marriage. One where we could learn to live with one another in a shared space and fulfil marital obligations and move on.

But no. James has sunk his way deep inside me. Into my heart. Into my soul. It turns out I was wrong. I don't just want to fulfil my obligation when it comes to James. I want to give him everything. I want him to know every part of me. Every wrongdoing, every lie I've ever told, everything. I've never wanted that with anyone else.

But with James? I want it all.

James

"HE WAS RUNNING naked across the commons!" Oliver is shrieking with delight while telling Marnie an old story from university.

"What I wouldn't have given to see that." She's

dabbing tears from her eyes as these two regale each other with stories about the both of us.

"They are too chummy," Zara whispers over her wine glass.

"Need I remind you, this was your doing." I throw an arm over her shoulder, bringing her closer to me.

"It's not my fault you're somewhat of a novelty and my friends want to meet you."

"Best friend," Marnie chimes in from across the table. "And yes, I have to make sure you're right for my best girl."

"And do I pass muster?" I take a sip of my scotch, leaning across the table. I don't back down from her intense gaze.

"That depends."

"On?" Would she stop beating around the bush and get to the point?

"On how you'll treat Zara. Do you plan on going back to your womanizing ways?"

I peer over at Zara, and a smile stretches across her lips. "Did you know about this?"

"Oh no. But knowing Marnie, it doesn't surprise me." She tips her wine glass in her direction, before leaning into me. "But if I were you, I'd answer her questions. You don't want to get on her bad side."

I swing my gaze from Zara to Marnie, and she presses again. "Well? You going to answer, pretty boy?"

"Of course I'm not going back to my womanizing ways." The accusation cuts deep. I'll be the first to admit that I wasn't a big fan of relationships. The less I knew about the women I slept with, the better. But not Zara. The thought of hurting her makes my chest physically ache.

"And how will you protect her from the paparazzi?" Marnie takes another sip of her drink. Oliver's eyes are bouncing back and forth between the two of us like he's watching a tennis match.

"He's already done that. Next question." Zara's warm hand lands on mine. I flip it over, clutching her hand to me. I don't have to look at her to know that she feels safe now whenever she leaves the safety of her house or school.

"Fine. Do you plan to cook for her?"

Bollocks.

"You do not want James in the kitchen. He burned spaghetti at uni."

"How in the world do you burn spaghetti?" This time, Zara forces my eyes to hers. Laughter fills her eyes. I love seeing how happy she is. It fills me with a sense of calm that I didn't know I wanted.

"I didn't put enough water in." My voice is quiet as I take a sip.

"You nearly burned down the house, mate!"

"Oy, shut it with the stories already!" I throw my napkin at Oliver. "I'm supposed to be winning over Marnie here."

"Oh darling, you won me over the second I heard all about the night at the symphony."

A blush creeps up Zara's face as I look at her. "You told her?" I grab her by the waist, hauling her into my lap.

"Not everything."

"Good. Because otherwise there might not be a repeat performance." I nibble on her earlobe, not caring about the company we're in.

"And on that note, I think you and I should head to the pub and get some more drinks." Oliver stands, pulling out Marnie's chair for her.

"That is a fab idea, Ollie."

"Cheers then, mates. Zara, you'll do just fine keeping

this wanker in line." Oliver winks at me as he guides Marnie out of the room.

"Piss off!" I shout behind his retreating back, then turn to Zara and vow, "I blame you for any stories that get leaked to the press tonight."

She nuzzles her face into my neck. "And why would that be my fault?"

"Because now they're friends, and Oliver is like a high-speed train anywhere he goes. Best to hold on and see what happens."

"At least you know we can all hang out and it won't be boring."

I squeeze Zara closer to me. The space between us at dinner was far too much. Shite, now I'm sounding like a bloody romantic arsehole.

"You should know by now, Zara, that it will never be boring with me."

Chapter Fourteen

"I promise, they'll love you." My voice is soft as I kiss along the shell of Zara's ear. I can't get enough of this woman. I've always been a one and done kind of man. Not something I'm proud of, but given my role in life, women only want one thing. And I was fine with that—until Zara came along. Now, all I want is her with me all the time.

"The last time I saw your mum I didn't exactly make the best first impression." She tilts her head just so, giving me better access. Her perfume lingers on the graceful slope of her neck. Christ, if we weren't on our way to lunch with my family, I'd take her right here. She's intoxicating.

"It wasn't the best day for either of us. This will be a much better meeting. Besides, they'll be so worked up over Ellie that they won't even pay us any attention." I drop a hot kiss where her shoulder meets her neck. The moan it elicits is downright dirty.

"Stop it. I don't want to look like two sex-starved people when we get there." Zara pushes me off of her, and I grumble a few choice words for her. "I want your family to like me."

"You've tamed me. How could they not like you?" I pull Zara into my arms as we inch closer to the palace. Being with her is the only place I want to be lately.

"Taming you and them liking me to be the future Queen of England are two very different things."

"And I assure you, they'll love you for both of those things." Almost as much as I do.

Bloody hell, where did that thought come from? It's too soon. I can't possibly be falling for the woman my mum set me up with, can I? But looking at this woman, curled into my side as we enter the palace gates, I know I'm falling hopelessly in love with her.

"Your Highness. Lady Zara. We're here." The driver pulls up and our door is opened, breaking the moment.

"Thank you." Zara's waiting for me as she steps out of the car. She looks absolutely stunning in the black trousers and jumper she chose to wear today. I can't wait to tear them off her later. Anything to distract myself from thoughts of falling in love with her.

"Shall we?" I give her my arm as I guide her into the palace.

Her eyes are everywhere as I lead her up a side staircase to the family quarters. The last time she was here, she came as a guest through the main corridor. This time, I'm taking her along a different route, but it's no less extravagant. The opulence on display here sometimes blows even me away.

"What's on your mind, love?" I squeeze her closer to me as we reach the top of the stairs. Family portraits from the centuries of rule stare down at us.

"Feels much different coming here this time than it did last time."

I turn, wrapping my arms around her. "There's

nothing to worry about. My sister will adore you in a heartbeat. Probably more than she does me."

Zara pulls me in close, resting her head on my shoulder. I love how perfectly she fits in my arms. Like she was made for me and only me.

"Let's get moving. The sooner we get this over with, the sooner I can take you back to my house and we can have our own fun." Her body shakes with laughter as she turns to look at me. Zara's eyes are happy. I love that I put that there.

"Alright, Prince Charming. Let's get going." She tugs my hand, as I'm helpless to follow her. I'd follow this woman anywhere, even if she's leading us in the wrong direction.

"This way, love." I tug her hand down the opposite hall, and she gives me a sheepish smile.

"There's too many halls here."

"I'll be sure to draw you a map when we move in."

Zara

LOUD VOICES from the end of the hall cause butterflies to erupt in my stomach. I don't know why I'm so nervous. I've already met the Queen once. It didn't turn out so well, but I'm still nervous to meet the rest of James's family. Can one pass out from nerves?

James tugs me through the open door, and I'm met with happy, smiling faces.

"The prodigal son returns." A woman with bright pink hair and a noticeable baby bump crushes James in a hug.

"What can I say, someone has to pick up the reins since you ditched us." She punches him in the stomach before fixing her gaze on me. "And you must be the famous Zara we've heard so much about. I'm this one's sister, Ellie."

"It's nice to meet you." I stick my hand out, but she brushes it aside, sweeping me in for a hug.

"I've heard so much about you. I can't believe you've managed to tame my brother." Her face is bright with playfulness.

"I don't think I like you talking to her." James appears behind Ellie's back.

"Nonsense. Go talk to Sean. I don't want Grandmum telling him anything inappropriate about birthing children."

His eyes go wide at that statement. "And you think I'd want to go join in on that conversation?"

Ellie gives him another hearty elbow to the ribs. "I want to talk to Zara. Off you go." She waves her hand to him as he sulks over to where Sean and their grandmum are. The Queen isn't here yet, so my nerves settle a bit.

"So Zara, how are things with James? From what I've been told, everyone seems to be loving the two of you together." We sit on the sofa in the sitting room. My entire house could fit in this room. Heavy drapes line the windows that open up to the back gardens and London's cloudy, lifeless skies. Newer photos of the family dot the furniture around the room.

"And what have you been told?" I give her a coy look.

"Only that everywhere the two of you go, you look like a couple in love."

"Gin and tonic?" James has a drink at the ready in front of me. It's like he knew I'd need one.

"Thank you." I give him a shy smile, not wanting to give any more ammunition to the rumours his sister is telling me about. He walks back over to Sean and his grandmum as I gulp down the drink.

"I believe that answers my question." Ellie leans back, rubbing her baby bump.

"How did that answer your question?" I'm confused as she just continues staring at me. It's unnerving. Ellie and James are mirror images of one another. Her bright pink hair is a contrast to James's dark waves, but they have the same bright blue eyes.

"He knew what you needed. There's this invisible thread connecting the two of you. Whether you choose to acknowledge it or not."

"It's still too early for that." I don't want to acknowledge my deepening feelings for James. It's scary, the world he lives in. I was hoping there wouldn't be any chemistry between the two of us and we could each continue living our lives. But the deeper I move into his world, the harder it is to reel in my emotions.

"Zara, it's never too early. I knew Sean was it for me within an hour of meeting him."

"An hour? You knew that soon he was the love of your life?"

Ellie nods her head. "Do you really think I'd give up my entire life for anything less than true love?" Her eyes get hazy as she drifts them to look at Sean. Their connection is palpable to anyone in the room as his eyes are drawn to hers.

"I'd say the feeling is mutual." I take another sip, trying to hide my smile.

"Just don't dismiss him because of this life. There's more than meets the eye with him. He's a good one."

"I know he is." She doesn't have to tell me twice. The

persona that James shows the public is vastly different than who he is with me. He's flirty and fun with the press. They eat him up. But in the quiet moments I get with him, he opens up to me. I see the real James. And I am easily falling for him.

"Zara, it's so wonderful to see you today." The Queen's voice pulls me away from Ellie, a smile painting her face.

"Your Majesty." I stand, dipping into a low curtsy.

"Please. It's Katherine. We're all family here." She gives me a quick peck on the cheek before turning her warm gaze on Ellie.

"And how's the little one?"

"Doing just fine." Ellie's hands rub her growing belly as her mum sits between us.

"Still not going to find out what it is?"

"Mum. I've told you several times, no. We want to be surprised."

The Queen turns her stern gaze at me. "I've even tried telling her—as her Queen—that she should find out, but it's no use. And don't you get any ideas about not finding out." She wags her finger in my direction.

I hide my chuckle behind my hand. "Of course. You'll be the first to know. But that's still down the road."

"And I thought it would be a few years away for me but here we are, my first grandbaby is on the way." Her excitement is palpable.

"Darling, stop bugging them for grandchildren." Prince Frederick approaches his wife, pulling her towards the door. "Lunch is ready if you would like to head to the dining room."

Katherine gives her husband a tender look as she follows him. I can't help but wonder if these two were a love match or an arranged marriage like James and me.

"Ladies, shall we escort you into the dining room?"

James and Sean appear before us. Sean helps Ellie, pulling her into his arms and dropping a chaste kiss on her lips.

"Can you two not do that in front of me?" James turns into me, burying his face in my neck.

"I think we've all seen enough of you plastered all over the tabloids, so get over it." Ellie doesn't turn to face him. She links her arm through Sean's, and they head off in front of us.

"She might have a point, you know." James's scent overwhelms me, as he drapes his arm across my shoulder, tugging me close.

"You're supposed to be on my side." His voice is a low growl.

I give him a smug look. "Well, you're all mine now. I don't want anyone else seeing any bits of you."

"I like the sound of that." Before he can kiss me, James's grandmother is walking up to us.

"Come sit by me, dear. I'd love to get to know you better." James's grandmother pulls me from his side. He gives me a consoling look before moving to sit by his sister and Sean.

The table is lined with several dishes, at least three different kinds of roasts, pudding, vegetables, and sides. They know how to do Sunday roast at the palace.

"Don't look so worried. I don't bite. At least not in a few years."

James's grandmother is a tiny human, but her reputation precedes her. The images of her at her husband's funeral showed a stoic woman without a tear in her eye.

"Would you get me another gin before you sit down, darling?" She hands me her glass, and I top her off before sitting beside her.

"What's a Sunday lunch without a little pick me up?" She smacks her lips after taking a hearty gulp.

"So right, ma'am." God, could I sound any more foolish calling James's grandmother ma'am?

"Zara, dear. Please do not call me ma'am. It's Minerva. Ma'am makes me sound old and fussy." Her wrinkly hand settles on my forearm as meals are distributed to everyone. "I've got a few years before I'm old and fussy."

"Sorry, Minerva."

"Now, how are things going with my grandson? Still have his head up his arse about this whole image thing?" She takes a bite of the roast and pierces me with a withering stare. I don't know what I expected from her, but it was definitely not this.

"I think he's been doing much better."

"Don't spin things for this old bat. I want the details." Shock must be written all over my face, because James is looking at me like he's ready to jump to my rescue. I give him a small smile before turning back to his grandmother.

"If it makes you feel better, I don't think there's been a single mention about his playboy ways in a few weeks."

She rolls her eyes at me. "Well, that's not exciting, now is it?"

"Isn't that the whole purpose of the two of us being together? To rehab his image?"

Minerva waves me off. "Where's the fun in that? My Edward and I used to get into all sorts of trouble together."

"Why don't I remember hearing about any of that?"

"Because we didn't have to worry about the paps like you do now. If you ever want to know about any of the hidden spots in palaces around the world, I'm your woman."

I almost choke around the bite I took. "I'll have to keep that in mind." The thought of getting sex advice from

James's grandmum? I can't think of anything more mortifying.

"You probably won't, but that's alright. I can see how happy you're making my grandson."

A flush creeps over my cheeks. "He makes me happy too."

Minerva pops another bite into her mouth. "From the pictures I've seen, you're quite the couple."

"You keep track of us in the tabloids?" I take a cooling sip of my own drink.

"A way to pass the time. I'm old, and most of my friends are gone. No one cares about me at this point, so why not see what's going on with others?" She shrugs her shoulders as if this is no big deal.

"I wish we didn't have to worry about them." The press lingering outside my house still makes me anxious.

"Comes with the territory. I have no doubt that you'll be able to handle them with all the dignity and grace that my grandson does." She squeezes my forearm before going back to her meal.

It's been an eye-opening afternoon. Being surrounded by all these people who love and adore James makes me fall that much harder. He's kind and caring. He makes me laugh, and I've never felt sexier or more desired than when I'm with him.

I never thought I'd fall in love with my fiancé, but here I am. Doing it just the same.

Chapter Fifteen

JAMES

"My grandmother didn't scare you off?" I follow Zara into her house. We spend more time here than we do at my apartment, but this feels like home. I know we won't be able to stay here once the engagement is official, but damn, if I don't love the feeling of being in her space.

"Apparently she was disappointed we don't have better stories for her." She shakes her head as she sinks down onto her sofa. I sit, pulling her feet into my lap.

"Better stories?" I take off her heels and dig my fingers into her soles of her feet.

"Oh God, that feels amazing." Her groan goes straight to my dick. As much as I'd love to take her right here, right now, I'm buttering her up.

"You didn't answer my question."

Zara drops her head back onto the couch. "She said that she and the King used to get into all sorts of trouble, but we never heard about it because it was never in the press."

"Goes to show you how times have changed. Also, let's not talk about that."

"You mean your grandmum and granddad doing dirty things to one another?" Her head pops up on a laugh. "If you ever want to know good spots for doing dirty things in palaces around the world, Minerva knows."

I cringe, pulling Zara closer to me. "Never say those words again. No one wants to know about that."

"She's your grandmum!" she says on a laugh, snuggling closer to me.

I wrap my arms around her, tilting my head to whisper in her ear, "Play for me, Z."

She pulls back, a blush crawling up her beautiful face. "Now?"

"No, in ten years." I roll my eyes. "Yes, now. I've never heard you play before."

"But my violin is in pieces." She looks down, toying with the hem of my jumper.

"I know you have another." I lift her chin up, forcing her eyes to meet mine. "Why don't you want to play for me?"

"Because I'm nervous. What if you don't like how I sound?"

I drop my forehead to hers. Christ, this woman is doing me in. "Zara, love. I will love anything you play for me. I just want to hear you play."

"You promise?" Her breath ghosts over my lips, and it almost distracts me from the issue at hand. Almost.

"Yes. Now, play for me. I don't care what."

Her lips capture mine. They taste like her drink from lunch earlier. When her tongue glides along the seam of my lips, I open for her. There's nothing I wouldn't give this woman. But just as fast as she kisses me, she pulls away.

She leaves the living room before coming back with her violin.

"Just don't be disappointed if it doesn't sound amazing. I haven't played with Henrietta in quite some time."

I nearly choke on a laugh. "You name your instruments?"

"Duh." She gives me an incredulous look before tuning it. I relax back into the couch, waiting until she takes a deep breath and settles the violin under her chin. Zara's eyes flip to mine, and I give her an encouraging nod before the first notes hit me.

I'm not a musician. I've never been into the arts, as that was always Ellie's thing. But hearing Zara play for me? I understand why people love music. The symphony has nothing on her.

The notes have a haunting quality to them as she starts to pick up speed. She sways in time with the notes as the music flows through me. It's fast then slow. Heavy and light all in the same breath.

Zara is absolutely breathtaking. She's a dream playing this song for me. I have no idea who wrote it, but I'll always remember it.

When she's done playing, her eyes are heavy. Hazy. It's like she was making love with the song, and damn, if that doesn't turn me on.

"Well?" She holds her violin in front of her, like she's guarding herself from criticism from me.

"I have no words." Her face drops for a moment before I stand and take a few quick steps and pull her into me. My lips are attacking hers with no finesse. I'm hungry for her. It's all teeth and tongues clashing. Hearing Zara play for me peeled back another layer to her. This person who is so passionate about her music and her life's calling to teach it.

"I have no words for how incredible that was, love." My thumbs tenderly brush her cheeks.

"Yeah?" Her voice is soft.

"Yes." I drop a kiss on her forehead. "It was beautiful." A kiss on her nose. "Better than the orchestra we went to." A ghost of a kiss on her lips.

She laughs, looking up into my eyes. Her brown eyes are swimming with warmth. "Now I know you're lying."

I smile against her lips. "Not a lie. I'd rather listen to you any day of the week, Zara."

She sets her violin down before wrapping her arms around me. "Did I tell you my mum taught me to play?"

I shake my head.

"She was a brilliant violinist. Also played the cello. I don't remember much about her since she died when I was little, but I remember her teaching me to play."

I squeeze her tighter to me. "And the violin that was destroyed was hers?"

She nods against me. "I know I shouldn't be so attached to it, but it's one of the last things I have left of hers."

I fucking hate that the paparazzi destroyed something so cherished by Zara. I don't know how I can make it right, but I have to fix her violin. No matter the cost.

"I know she would be so proud of you." Zara's face is soft as she turns those gorgeous brown eyes on me that I can get lost in. "You are pretty incredible." I run my hands down her cheeks, before placing a chaste kiss on her lips.

She steps out of my arms, biting down on her lip. God, she's the sexiest woman I've ever met. She wraps her hand in mine. No words are said as she leads me upstairs to her bedroom. It's dark, the curtains blocking out any light from the houses behind hers. Zara stops in the centre of her room, and I step into her space, letting my fingers drift lazily up her arms.

An anticipation like I've never known buzzes through me. Zara's hands grasp my waist as I trail hot, wet kisses up her neck to her jaw. I linger, nibbling just how she likes, before moving to her lips. She opens for me the second my lips are on hers. The soft tangle of our tongues makes my dick impossibly hard. I've never known a need like this before. I crave her with every fibre of my being.

Her warm hands fist in my shirt as I guide us back to the bed. She sits, looking up at me with all the love in the world. Fuck, this woman is absolutely doing me in. Pulling my jumper and T-shirt off, I kneel in front of her. My hands drift up her legs, stopping where she's trying to get friction. I pull her forward and lift her jumper over her head. Pushing her back, I trail warm kisses up her soft stomach.

Zara is arching into my touch. Her nipples are diamond hard through the lacy cups of her bra. Teasing her, I run my fingertip over the tight bud of one nipple while sucking on the other through the fabric.

"James." Her voice is husky, laced with want. I pull back, hovering above her. Lightning trails through my body as her fingers drag down my chest, hooking into the waistband of my jeans.

Our eyes lock. Her brown eyes are dark with need and lust and want. And love. There is so much love shining out of them that I don't feel worthy of it. Instead of dwelling on these new emotions that Zara is bringing out in me, I crush my lips to hers.

The soft, wet heat of her mouth is driving me crazy. We battle for control as our tongues sweep into each other's mouths. I don't remember kissing ever being this good. There's something about Zara that overwhelms me.

I flip onto my back, and she deepens the kiss, grinding over my rock-hard dick. I love that she takes control like this, but I want her naked and writhing beneath me.

"Mmm, Zara." All thought leaves my mind as her lips trail down my neck and chest. I should stop her once she gets to my jeans, but I don't. Her soft hands unzipping and pulling them down my body is too much, yet not enough at the same time.

My cock springs free, precum dripping from the tip. Her smile is downright evil as she licks me from base to head, swirling her tongue about the crown. "Fuck, Zara. That feels too damn good."

She takes me to the back of her mouth, and I can't help thrusting up. She gags but doesn't stop. Her eyes are hooded with lust as she continues sucking and licking me, playing with my balls. Fire is racing down my spine as my release threatens. Threading my hands through Zara's silky locks, I pull her off me with a pop.

"I'm not ready to come in your mouth. I want to be buried inside of you as I make you come."

Zara stands, dropping her bra, and her gorgeous tits are put on display for me. "Damn, you are so fucking sexy." I pull Zara down onto the bed, stripping her of the rest of her clothes. Her pussy is glistening for me. Swiping my finger through the wetness, I drag it down towards the tight pucker of her arsehole. She squirms into my touch.

"You like that? You want me to fuck this gorgeous arse of yours?"

"Yes, James! God yes!" Her voice carries around the quiet room as I dip down and take her clit in my mouth.

"Your wish is my command, my Queen."

I continue sucking on her clit, ignoring the aching throb in my dick. Thrusting two fingers inside her hot, wet channel, I bring her closer to orgasm. Zara is writhing beneath me as her pussy starts clenching around me, her release coating my fingers. I don't relent as I stay on her until she comes down.

Her skin is flushed from her orgasm. I lean back on my heels, her sated body laid out before me. She's beauty in its purest form.

"Do you have any lube?" My voice is husky. I'm ready to explode and have to stroke myself a few times to hold back my release.

"Bathroom cabinet. Bottom drawer."

I waste no time finding exactly what I need and returning to Zara. She's up on her elbows, watching me jog back to her.

"Someone's eager." She's got a condom in her hand that I pluck out, rolling it down my hard length. Coating my fingers with lube, I rub it up and down my cock, before I spread her legs apart.

"Fuck. You look so sexy laid out like this for me." I slowly push a finger inside as she takes a deep breath. Getting past the tight ring of muscle, she relaxes against me. "That's it, love. You're doing great."

Zara takes my finger to the knuckle as I start moving in and out of her. Her groans tell me she's ready for another finger. I want to make this as good for her as possible.

"How is it possible that this feels so good?" Her voice is breathy as she bears down on my fingers. Knowing she's ready, I pull my fingers out and line my cock up.

"If you want to stop, just tell me." I lean down over her, resting my forehead against hers.

"I'm ready."

I skim her lips with kisses as I push inside, giving her a moment to adjust. Once she starts moving underneath me, I push all the way in, inch by slow inch.

I have to silently sing "God Save the Queen" so I don't

blow my load immediately. It's heaven. Nothing has ever felt better than being inside Zara like this. She consumes me as I start moving, shallow thrusts at first. But the more she moves under me, the faster I go. Hiking one leg over my shoulder, I deepen the angle.

"James. I'm so close. So damn close." She's chewing on her bottom lip as a bead of sweat trails down her temple. I pick her other leg up and wrap it around my waist. I watch, my own orgasm racing down my spine, as Zara starts massaging her clit.

"Fuck. I need you to come right now." Thrust. "I'm not going to last much longer." My thrusts are hard and unrelenting as Zara starts to come apart around me. Her screams of ecstasy take me over the edge with her. I pump my release into the condom as I start to still above Zara. She holds me to her as I collapse on top of her. There is no better feeling in the world than being wrapped in this woman's arms.

The thundering of her heart under my head matches my own. It has nothing to do with what we just did and everything to do with the woman I did it with. I've gone and fallen irrevocably in love with my future Queen.

Chapter Sixteen

ZARA

"Why do I feel like I'm back in primary school and being summoned to the headmaster's office?" For once, James and I didn't have any plans. No events. No galas. Nothing. We were going to have a lazy Sunday afternoon at his house. But a call came from the Queen, requesting our presence at the palace.

"Because whenever the Queen wants to see you, there's usually a reason," James answers.

James pulls into the gates of Buckingham. The last time I was here, I was nervous. But after getting to know James's family better, I feel more comfortable here.

"Did she tell you why we needed to come here today?" James grabs my hand as we head inside.

"We'll find out," James says, his face uneasy.

"Your Highness. Lady Zara. The Queen's advisor greets us. "James. Your mother is waiting for you in her quarters. Miss Cross, please come with me."

"I guess I'll meet you back here when we're done?" James says as he turns to me, his brow creased in confusion.

"Sounds good." He drops a quick kiss on my lips before leaving me behind.

"Please, follow me, miss."

I follow the advisor, heading deeper into the palace. She opens a heavy set of wooden doors, and the perfumed smell of flowers greets me.

"Lady Zara. It's a pleasure to meet you." A woman in a form-fitting red dress greets me. "I'm Thea and I will be assisting you with the wedding plans."

"Wedding plans?" I can't hide the shock in my voice.

"Yes. We need to get started with plans, as there will be a lot of moving parts on the day of."

"But we're not even engaged yet!" My voice comes out higher than I expected.

"Not to worry. That will be taken care of soon."

"Taken care of soon?" James and I have been seeing each other for a few months. An engagement is not something that should be "taken care of."

"Yes. Your engagement should be announced within the next two months, so it's best we start preparations now."

The room is getting hot around me, the heavy perfume of the flowers doing nothing to help. I never thought much about my wedding growing up. Not having a mum made it hard to think about my wedding. I always wished I had my mum here to share in my special day. Not some tightly wound royal wedding planner.

"We'll need to decide on flowers and cake today. Dresses will be for a later time, once we have a list of approved designers to choose from." So much for the magic of planning your wedding.

"Shouldn't James be here for this?" The grand room we're in is filled to the brim with flowers. Cakes that are taller than I am line one wall.

Thea laughs, pinning me with a look that tells me this is for women only. Figures. "He is otherwise preoccupied. Now, if you'll please come with me."

I follow her farther into the room. "Now, the flowers will need to make a statement," Thea starts. "Orchids and roses are acceptable. We don't want anything too out there. We don't want to offend anyone."

"Heaven forbid the flowers I choose for my wedding offend anyone."

Thea gives me a piercing glare, her tight bun making her features even more harsh. "A great deal of research has been done as to the proper bouquets for royals. One misstep and everyone will remember your wedding for those reasons."

I try to listen as Thea goes into far more detail than I ever needed to know about flowers, but my mind is spinning. When James and I were summoned to the palace today, I never thought it would be to start planning my wedding.

"Zara? Which of these do you like?" Thea sweeps her hands to four different bouquets laid out in front of me. All are a combination of white flowers. The differences are subtle.

I chew on my bottom lip. There has to be a test in here somewhere. Did they put the unacceptable flowers in here to see if I would pick the right one? Why is there so much pressure on this one decision?

"Am I able to decide later?" My voice is hardly a whisper.

"I'm afraid the flowers and cake must be decided upon today. To get everything scheduled for a royal wedding requires quite a bit of time." Thea's voice is curt. From the look she's giving me, I doubt she likes me very much.

"How about this one?" I grab the one closest to me.

"I think this one would be best." She points a different one out to me.

"Then that one will be fine." I don't know why I'm needed here. It makes no difference to me which flowers or cake I have at my wedding. If Thea is just going to tell me my decision is wrong and guide me towards the correct decision, I really don't need to be here.

"Fab. We will incorporate these flowers throughout the abbey and will also have them as the boutonniere flowers."

I give her a small smile as she leads me in the direction of the cakes.

"You'll love getting to taste these cakes. Some of Britain's best bakers have been hard at work these last few weeks to prepare these for you."

"How is this not all over the tabloids right now?" Cakes of all different shapes and sizes are laid out before me. Some are lined with gold leaves, others with intricate flowers covering them.

"We have very strict policies as to who we can work with. All sign non-disclosure agreements. If it were leaked, we'd know."

I guess there can be one good thing to be said for being a royal.

"Want to have a taste?" Thea's face is in direct conflict with mine. Whereas she is beaming, I'm dreading this.

I try to put on a happy face, but this is just a bit overwhelming for me.

"Just tell me where to start."

James

"Mother. What did I do to be beckoned to the palace today?"

"Why must it be anything bad?" She gives me a peck on the cheek. As I move to sit down, she grabs my arm, leading me in the opposite direction.

"Where are we going?" I have a guess as to where we're going, but a feeling of dread starts to wash over me.

"Well, with the engagement being announced soon, it's about time we got Zara a ring, don't you think?"

"Mum! We've barely been dating a few months!" My voice echoes around the empty hall.

She stops, turning to face me. "James. You knew what was going to happen when you met Zara. You can't tell me you're surprised by this."

I open and close my mouth, like a gaping fish. "But things have been going well for the two of us. I guess I just assumed that maybe you might back off this whole arranged marriage thing."

"If I were to back off, you'd likely dump that kind girl in a heartbeat and be out at the clubs within the hour."

"Ouch. Thanks, Mum." I turn away from her, scrubbing my hand down my face. As crazy as it sounds, I haven't wanted to go to the clubs in weeks. Not when I have Zara. But does she really deserve to be brought into this crazy life?

"You've been doing a marvellous job lately, and I have no doubt it's thanks to Zara. But this marriage is moving forward as planned." Her tone leaves no room for argument. Her no-nonsense attitude causes my blood to boil.

"Fine, Mum. Lead the way." My jaw ticks in anger. My teeth could crack I'm so upset.

Following Mum down to the vaults here at the palace, I

try to push my anger aside. The vaults are dark, lights shining on the jewels inside.

"I've taken the liberty to pick a few out that Zara might like."

"Of course you have," I mutter under my breath.

I walk over to her, looking at the rings laid out before me. Christ, I'm really doing this, aren't I?

"All of these have been in the family for centuries. It will be the perfect ring to symbolize the past but also signify a new future for the two of you."

"I thought my past is what got us in this situation." Bitterness undercuts my tone.

"There's no need to be rude, James."

I slam my hand down on the table in front of me. "And there was no need to ambush me today about picking our engagement rings, but here we are."

"Will you please excuse us?" Mum motions to the guards behind her and they leave. Once they're gone, she fixes me with a look that could strike down a lesser man. A lesser man wouldn't be gearing up for a fight today.

"You need to lose this attitude. Like I said before, you've come a long way since Zara has entered your life, and solidifying your union will secure your place in the eyes of our country as a steadfast King. I will not hear another word about it."

I screw a fake smile on my face. "Fine, Mum. Being forced to pick out an engagement ring when I was hoping I could do this down the road on my own sounds brilliant." I turn to look at the rings laid out before me. "This one should do." I don't even care what it looks like.

I know I'm acting like a child, but when Mum keeps shoving her agenda down my throat, I can't help it. If they want to have me pick a ring for Zara that means nothing to me, I'll do it. Zara would love the stories behind these rings, but there is no way I'm going to give her something that I was forced to pick by my mum.

"Are you actually going to look at any of them?" Mum's voice is angry now.

"I looked. This one is fine. Do you have ideas as to when I should propose? How?"

It's a shitty comment, but at this point, I'll do anything to be dismissed from her presence.

"We'll be announcing your engagement in a few months. How you want to do it before then is up to you."

"Is that all then?"

She turns, giving me a soft look. "I'm just looking out for you. When you're a parent, you'll understand."

I don't give her another word, turning my back on her and leaving the vault. I know my behaviour back there was appalling, but Mum just brings it out in me. I was hoping that with time, I could do this on my own.

The more I've gotten to know Zara, the more I wanted to be able to do this the right way. I wanted to talk with Marnie and find the perfect ring for her. Plan an elaborate ruse to make her think I'm going to propose, but then do it in the quiet of our home.

But it's tainted now. Tainted by Mum forcing rings upon me. Pushing our dates up. Zara and I are doing so well, and I hate to think what she's going to think of all this.

Zara is pacing in front of the car when I find her. "Ready to go?"

"Yes." She wastes no time getting in. If I was bombarded with ring options, I can only imagine what her day was like.

"Want to talk about it?" I put the car in gear, wanting to put as much distance between the palace and us as possible.

"Did you know there is such a thing as an offensive flower?"

Christ. Her day was just as bad as mine. "I'm assuming you know all about it?"

She turns, her face not showing any of the usual emotion I've come to find from her. "Yes. And I know all about the different kinds of cakes and what is appropriate for a royal wedding."

"Bloody hell. I can't believe this is happening."

"Oh, it's happening. The flowers and cake Thea chose for our big day will be wonderful." Her tone is caustic. "'Zara, please choose which flowers you'd like, but oh, not that one because it might offend some people. And choco-late cake might stain your dress. We can't have that.'" She mimics this Thea person she's talking about.

"I can't believe she did this."

I go to grab Zara's hand, but she pulls it away from me. "Can you just take me home? I'm just overwhelmed right now and need to be alone."

I don't want her closing herself off, but given my own mood, I can't blame her. It just hurts more than it should. What started as a nice afternoon with Zara has turned into a nightmare. I can only hope this wedge between us goes away. Because whether we like it or not, this wedding is happening. And possibly sooner than we both had hoped.

Chapter Seventeen

"Are you sure I'm dressed appropriately for this?" Looking down at my stylish blazer, jeans, and wedge heels, I'm not so sure I'm going to fit in. After the week James and I had, it's nice to be out in a neutral environment. Neither one of us wanted to talk about being bombarded with the wedding at the palace, but it's been a cloud hanging over us. The pressure facing both of us at our pending nuptials isn't something we want to think about.

"Are you planning on trying out for the team?" James's heated stare moves up and down my body. "I'd give you the captain's position without question."

I smack his hard chest. "Of course you would."

James pulls me into his side before we walk out of the tunnel. "You look sexy as sin. Trust me, today it's all about George and his family meeting the team. They won't even know we're here."

"And he just thinks he's getting a tour of the stadium?" James told me all about the sweet boy he met touring the hospital. Seeing how happy he was to make this happen caused my heart to flutter.

"Yes. He has no idea he's meeting the team and will get to go to the match tonight."

I pull James to a stop, tucked away in the darkness of the tunnel. "He is going to lose his mind." Wrapping my arms around James's neck, I drop a sweet kiss on his lips.

"Maybe I can make you lose your mind tonight." His breath ghosts over my lips. Rolling my lips between my teeth, I stifle the moan that wants to escape.

"One thing at a time." Patting his chest, I walk towards the growing voices.

"This place is brilliant!" The excited voice of a young boy floats towards us.

"Do we get to go out onto the pitch?"

"C'mon, love. Let's go give him the surprise of his life." James grabs my hands and drags me away from the dark cove we were hidden away in.

"Mr. and Mrs. Smythson. George. Victoria. I'm so happy you all could join us today." James shakes hands with the parents before getting down on George's level. A bright blue cast hugs his leg in the wheelchair. "Are you excited today?" George is wearing his best Chelsea jersey and hat. I've never seen a brighter smile on anyone in my life.

"I can't wait to see where they play! I just wish I didn't have to be in this wheelchair," his voice squeaks out.

"It's easier for you to get around, love. You'll still get to see everything." His mum pats him on the shoulder.

"Well, what are you waiting for? Let's go!" James grabs the chair and wheels him down the tunnel.

"What's your name?" The dark-haired girl stands back as James leads us all out onto the field.

"I'm Zara. And you're Victoria?"

She nods at me. "I'm not a big football fan."

I bend down on her level, sticking my hand out to her. "Want to know a secret? I'm not a big football fan either."

"You're not?" She grins. "I like music more."

"I do too." Victoria chats my ear off as we follow everyone out onto the pitch. "I love the piano. But I'd love to learn the cello. And the flute. Lizzo plays the flute."

"Maybe you could be the next Lizzo."

"No way!" George's excited voice carries through the quiet stadium. "The players are here?"

"Prince James, this is too much." Mrs. Smythson is almost in tears as James gives them a big smile. The players jog over, crowding around George. A few of the trainers and coaches are with them.

"Do you want to meet them while we're here?"

For not liking football, Victoria seems a little starstruck. I walk her over, and the players swarm around her too. Stepping back, I let the family have their moment.

Looking around to find James, he's talking with one of the coaches. One of the female coaches. Jealousy flares up deep inside me. I shouldn't let it bother me. The connection between James and me is real. At least I thought it was real. It's been real for me.

And when she touches his arm? James gives her his thousand-watt smile. My stomach falls to my feet. It doesn't mean anything. Even though it's been a weird week for the two of us, I know what we feel for each other.

James is always affable with everyone he meets, but for the first time, his past slams into our present. Into our future. Is this what it is going to be like? Women flirting and throwing themselves at him everywhere we go? There's no way I can compete with the likes of these women.

"What do you say? Want to be our special guest

tonight?" George's loud shriek pulls me out of my morose thoughts. James catches my glance and gives me a wink. Instead of settling me, it just puts me more at odds with my emotions. Here is this incredible man, doing this amazing thing for this family after meeting them at the hospital. And all I can think about is how that woman was flirting with James. And he wasn't doing anything to stop it.

"Can we, Mum?" George turns eager eyes to his parents.

"Of course we can, darling." She rubs his shoulder, and the team cheers for him.

"Alright, how about a tour of the locker rooms?" George starts wheeling himself out of the centre of the huddle and follows a few players, chatting their ears off about plays. It's nice to see both of these siblings are passionate.

"Well, I'd say that went very well." James comes over to me, throwing his arm over my shoulder. The woman he was talking to gives him the side-eye, but he doesn't pay her any mind. Maybe it's all in my head. But James has always been called the Playboy Prince, and it's hard to shake that image. Women throw themselves at him, and maybe it's something I need to get used to. But if this has any chance at working, I need to accept that and move on.

"You're great with kids." I wrap my arm around his hips as we bring up the rear of the group. "James. This is what you should do for your patronage."

We're in the middle of the pitch when James stops, looking around him. "Bringing kids I meet in hospital to their favourite football club?"

"No, you wanker. Kids and sports. This is for one kid. Think of how many amazing things you could do for more children."

The wheels are turning. "You really think this could work?"

I grab his hands, giving them a firm squeeze. "You're so good with kids. And you have access to places that most people would only dream about. Why not combine the two?"

"Would you be there to help?" James pouts his lips at me. "I don't know if I could do it without you."

His tone is vulnerable. It quiets my doubts about him. "James, everyone was enraptured by you today. You have so much power to do good in this world."

James wraps his arms around me, settling his head in the crook of my neck. A heavy breath leaves his lips. "You're the first person to ever have so much confidence in me."

Shock slams into me. "There's no way that's true."

"Do you know what it's like to be the spare? The bar was set so low for me, that eventually there was no bar."

"So you just started doing whatever you wanted."

"Yes. Clubs. Women. I really didn't give a flying fuck what I was doing." James lets go of me, pacing in front of me. "It was all about Ellie. And don't get me wrong, I love my sister, but if they weren't grooming her to take over the throne, then it wasn't on their radar."

James looks so small walking around this massive field. "Where is all this coming from?" I ask softly.

"I'm just tired of the fucking paparazzi dredging up my past. When do I get a fresh start? When do *we* get a fresh start?"

"Hey." Placing a hand on his chest, I stop him and his racing thoughts. "What makes you think we didn't get a fresh start?"

His heart is racing under my palm. "Because you wouldn't be here if we did."

"Ouch."

"Look, I really don't want to talk about this right now. Let's just go enjoy the rest of our afternoon with the Smythsons." Shoving his hands in his pockets, James stalks away from me.

His mood is giving me whiplash today. He is his usually sparkling self one minute, and then worrying about our entire future in the next breath. James's shoulders are slumped as he heads back into the bowels of the stadium.

What in the world just happened?

James

THE MATCH SHOULD BE HOLDING my attention. It's tied two-two with ten minutes remaining, but all I can think about is the conversation with that coach earlier. I'm used to women hitting on me. But the way she propositioned me this afternoon even though Zara was there? It left a bad taste in my mouth.

She said she assumed I'd be down for a shag because I'd fucked so many other women before. Her words, not mine. And then Zara telling me she had faith in me? I couldn't handle it.

I wish I could sit here with George and talk strategy, but he's cheering his little head off. At least someone's day has been made. Zara has been an absolute charmer all afternoon. After we finished the tour, we were given a private box, and she kept Victoria entertained.

Zara has fit so seamlessly into my life that I didn't think

twice about it. But now, my past is kicking my arse. I should've known better than to expect everything to fall into place.

"Goal!" The crowd erupts around me as George stretches his hand up for a high five.

"That was the best goal I've ever seen!" His excitement is infectious. It's hard not to be when someone is this energized. "Did you see that, Prince James?"

"I did. It was excellent." Players are celebrating on the field as the crowd goes wild. Looking over at Zara, even she and Victoria are cheering along. She shoots me a smile as we go back to watching the end of the game. Chelsea squeaks out a win over a tough team.

"This was the best day ever!" George's voice is happier than I've ever heard someone.

"Prince James, we can't thank you enough for everything you've done for George. You've truly made his dreams come true." Mrs. Smythson is giving me a warm smile. "I don't think anything will ever live up to meeting his heroes today."

"I'm glad I could give him this experience. It's given me a lot of great ideas."

"What sort of ideas?" Her husband has left her to help move George along, still talking about the match.

"Just thinking of how this could maybe become a new project of mine. Broaden the reach and help more children. Not just things like this, but bringing sports to areas that may not have the funds to support local teams."

Her face lights up with a smile. "That is absolutely brilliant. I can only imagine how many children will benefit from that. I know George is itching to get back to playing."

"Hopefully he'll get his cast off soon." He had me sign it before, but it didn't compare to having all his favourite players sign it.

"Are you ready to head home, Victoria?" She's still talking Zara's ear off as they walk over.

"Mum. I have all sorts of new songs I want to try. Can we go to the music store tomorrow?"

"Of course, love." She runs a hand down her daughter's hair in a loving manner. "Thank you again, Prince James, for such a wonderful afternoon and evening. Everyone is so happy."

"Thanks, James! This was brilliant. No one at school is going to believe I got to meet the players. They'll all be so jealous!"

"Now George, we don't want to go bragging. You wouldn't like it if your friends did that." His father takes a tone that sounds just like Mum's. Christ, is there a school all parents attend to master that?

"Thank you again, Your Highness." Mr. Smythson shakes my hand as they all head out. George is recapping the entire match on their way out as Victoria rolls her eyes. It's reminiscent of Ellie and me.

"What are you thinking about?" Zara wraps her arms around my waist, resting her chin on my shoulder.

"Just reminds me of Ellie and me when we were little."

I pull her in front of me. It's been a weird night, and these feelings floating up inside me don't have anywhere to go. I love this woman, but it seems no matter what I do, my past will always be rearing its ugly head to remind me why I'm in this situation with Zara. Doesn't she deserve better than a man who can't escape his womanizing past?

"You alright? You seem off today." That's one way of putting it.

"Taking stock of a few things. Nothing to worry about, love."

"Pretty heavy for a night at a football match." Zara drags the tips of her fingers over my cheek, before sliding into the hair at my neck. Her fingers rub soothing circles there. Fuck, what was I thinking about?

"Want to go back to your place and make it unheavy?"

She laughs at me. "Wow, what a charmer you are. You must get all the ladies with that line."

It stings, but I don't let her see that. "Why don't you charm me then?"

"Mmm, that sounds like a nice idea. Want to come back to my place and make it unheavy?" She throws my words back at me.

"Consider me charmed. Now let's get moving."

Chapter Eighteen

"And how is my favourite son doing today?" Dad's voice precedes him into my office.

"Mum sent you?" I sigh, dropping the pen in my hand. Since Mum called us to the palace last week, I haven't talked to her. Every time I think about what she did, I'm seething with anger.

"Can't I just come for lunch?"

"Fine. Can we make it quick? I've got a lot of work to do." After Zara's idea about the new charity, I hit the ground running. It's the only thing that I've been able to focus on lately. It's the perfect distraction with a very real wedding staring me down.

"I've already called down to the kitchen. Should be here soon." Dad sits in the chair across from my desk. "What are you working on?"

"It's a proposal for a new charity I want to start. There's a lot of fine details to work out, but I'm hoping it'll pass muster with Mum."

Dad gives me a quizzical stare. "You're serious about this."

"I wouldn't be doing it otherwise." It also made me realize how much I still have to learn.

"Zara's been a good influence on you."

A smile I can't control spreads across my face. Just the thought of Zara has my pulse quickening. No woman has ever made me feel like this. "She has. I know it wasn't the most orthodox situation, but she's fit herself quite nicely into our world."

The door to my office opens and lunch is wheeled in. I didn't realize how hungry I was until just now. I give a slight nod as the staff leaves us.

"Your mum is quite pleased." My dad brings us back to the conversation we were having.

A sigh slips out before I can stop it. "Is she though? It just seems that every step forward is two steps back, and that I'll never live up to this standard she has set for me."

The clank of his silverware dropping has my eyes meeting his. It's like looking into a mirror when I get to his age. I'm the spitting image of him. "I'm not saying this to upset you. We're both quite pleased, shocked really, at how quickly you took to this whole situation. We thought there would be more pushback from you."

"Because who expects to actually fall in love with the person they're arranged to be wed to?"

Bloody hell, did that just slip out? I haven't even told Zara I love her, and now I'm blabbing to my dad. The smile on his face tells me he didn't miss my slipup.

"You two remind me of your mum and me at your age. Except of course we had twin babies to look after."

"Does that mean there's hope for me yet?" A wave of relief rolls through me. I can't be doing that badly if I remind my dad of himself.

"There was never a loss of hope. If it seemed that way, it's because your mother has the weight of the common-wealth on her shoulders. We've always been in your corner. And with this new charity you plan on starting, the rest of the nation will be as well."

I feel like I'm fifteen again, wanting my dad's approval. I'm almost thirty for Christ's sake, but it feels like another piece is falling into place. Whereas before they were all scattered, now it finally feels like I'm settling into who I'm meant to be. To become.

My throat is tight with emotion when I squeeze out the words, "Thanks, Dad."

He gives me a brief nod, trying to control his own emotions. "I didn't just come here to get on you. Your mother has requested Zara to attend the Garden Show with us tomorrow."

Of course she has. I haven't picked up her call, so she sends Dad in her place, knowing I'd refuse her.

"But it's a school day. She'll have class all day." Her nights and weekends are already dominated by events I'm dragging her to. I don't want to disrupt her life any more than it has been.

"It'll be a good opportunity for her to get to meet more of her citizens. See more of what will be required of her when everything is made official."

"I'll call her once we're done," I relent. I know this will eventually be her reality, but I want her life to be as normal as possible until then. Even if her version of normal has shifted.

Finishing up lunch, Dad stands to go. I stand with him, but before he can leave, I pull him in for a hug. "Thanks, Dad."

He squeezes me in a little tighter. "I'm proud of you, James, and I know your grandfather would be too." He pulls back, giving my shoulder a squeeze before leaving. Fuck if my emotions aren't getting the best of me today.

When our grandfather was alive, Ellie was the one expected to eventually be on the throne. She was always the one that was given the attention. I hate to admit it, but it's one of the reasons I slacked off. There was never any pressure on me. I was never going to be leading the country. But now that I am, hearing those words affects me more than I thought they would. My grandfather was arguably the best King our country has ever seen, so to have those words said to me? My heart swells in my chest. And the only person I want by my side when I do this is Zara.

I need to hear her voice. Even if it is to invite her to another event.

"Hi." Her voice is muffled when she answers.

"Bad time?"

"Sorry, just trying to finish eating before lunch hour is over."

Here I am, worried about pulling her away from school when I'm calling her in the middle of the day. "Sorry, love. But just have a quick ask."

"Is it about the Garden Party tomorrow?"

"You're in the wrong profession if you guessed that." Shock colours my voice. How in the world would she know about that already?

"It's the same time every year, so I only assumed I'd be going. Good press for the two of us." She sighs. "Is that why you're calling?"

"You don't have to come if you don't want to. I can tell the Queen to bugger off."

This gets a laugh out of her. "I'm not going to make you tell your mother to bugger off, even if I'd like to tell her that right now. I've already requested the day off. I'm just worried because the week after is our end of term concert and I want to get all the practise time in with the students that I can."

She doesn't have to say it, but I know what she's thinking. That as soon as we get engaged, she'll have to quit her job. That she'll no longer get to teach music but will start training for her new role as princess. I hate that I'm taking her away from her life, but at the same time, I want her by my side.

"You're wonderful, you know that?"

She laughs, soothing the sting to my soul. "So you've told me. Do I just need to come to your place tomorrow?"

"If you want to come early, we can do lunch."

"Mmm, sounds like the start to a perfect day."

More like the perfect life.

Zara

"WOW, do I love a man in uniform." James opens the door in full military dress. I never thought I was one for a man in uniform, but apparently, I am. Or maybe it's just James. He's swoon-worthy in the black coat with white belt. "Did you earn all of these?" Medals decorate his chest.

"Some I did, but some were handed down at the behest of the King. But I'm most proud of the ones I earned in service." His voice is proud as he sweeps me in for a kiss.

"I'm thinking you might need to wear this more often," I whisper against his lips, trailing my fingers down the brass buttons of his uniform.

"You aren't looking so bad yourself, Miss Cross." His

eyes trail down my flowing dress, which is a light sage colour with a scalloped hem that hits just above my knees. It has plenty of spin to it for the warm summer day. The fascinator, complete with feathers and a mesh twist, is intricately woven into my hair.

"I wish we didn't have to go to this event. I could stay here with you all afternoon." My words are heated. I love this side that James brings out in me.

"If you aren't too tired, I plan on bringing you back here and doing exactly what you're thinking about right now."

"Then you best feed me now so I don't faint this afternoon." James grabs my hand, pulling me into the kitchen. A simple spread of sandwiches and crisps are spread out.

"Anything else to drink?" James hands me a water bottle as he sits next to me.

I shake my head. "I'm fine. So tell me, what can I expect this afternoon? All the pictures make it seem like such a high-end affair."

James's laugh echoes around the large kitchen. "Not as high-end as you would imagine. Today is in honour of the vets who served, so it will be the Queen shaking hands and meeting everyone. We'll be doing some of that, but not on Mum's level."

"Will you know anyone there?" I point to his uniform. "You know, since you served?"

He shakes his head, finishing the bite he shoved in his mouth. "No. These are typically higher-ups, and I never made that rank before I finished my service. You can only go so far in military service if you're royal. I went into active war zones, which is not typical for royals."

"Why did you get to serve?" I finish the sandwich I have and grab another. I can't say I'll mind the perk of having others cook for me.

"Because I was third in line to the crown. If I was second, I never would have gotten to serve in the Middle East. I'm so proud of my service and was humbled to do it, but if I tried to do it now, I'd be laughed away."

I cover his hand with mine. He turns his to take mine. It's an instinct. Whenever I reach for him, he holds on tight. I love the feel of his hand encasing mine. His warmth spreads through me. "I'm glad you got to serve."

James brings my hand to his lips, dropping kisses on each knuckle. "It's the one thing I'm proudest of. I'll be the first to admit, I've made some poor decisions in the past, but not about that."

"I'm glad I'll get to see a glimpse of that world today."

James tugs me closer to him. "Well then, we best finish up here and get a move on. It's good form to never keep the Queen waiting."

FROM THE MOMENT we arrived at the palace, James was whisked away. We had a few moments together when we entered behind the Queen, but I feel so out of place. Standing on the sides in the massive outdoor space, nerves are flowing like electricity through me. It seems everyone here knows someone but me.

I'm trying not to hide, but with the large crowd, I blend in.

"Can you believe he brought that excuse for a woman?" My ears perk up at a group of women who are at a nearby table.

"She's a poor excuse for a girlfriend. I can't believe James is dating her."

My stomach drops to my feet.

"It'll be over before the holidays. He knows how good we were together. They look terrible together in the news." A passing waiter offers me another glass of champagne, and I use it as an excuse to get a good look at these women.

Blonde hair, tight dresses, overly done makeup. The exact opposite of my tall, willowy frame.

Pricks of wetness coat my eyes. Will it always be like this? Women cutting me down because James chose me?

But he didn't choose you. That small voice of self-doubt kicks in. Just because our parents cooked up this whole arranged marriage doesn't mean I love James any less. Because I've fallen deeply in love with him these last few weeks.

It just worries me that he doesn't feel the same way. We've gotten closer than I ever thought we would, but is it all a ruse to him? The thought cuts through my heart.

"Excuse me, Zara?" A beautiful, curvy woman with long, dark hair and olive skin comes up to me, breaking through my morose thoughts. Red lipstick stains her lips. She's stunning.

"Yes, hi." I extend the free hand, the one not clutching my champagne glass like it's a lifeline.

"I'm Charlotte, James's cousin. You looked like you needed someone to talk to."

I blow out a deep breath. The sun is beating down on me, sweat prickling on my back. "Yes. I'm still learning the ropes, and it's quite unsettling."

Charlotte links her arm through mine. Her shoulders are exposed in her white sleeveless dress that billows around her ankles. A colourful fascinator adds several inches to her height. "It's very overwhelming some days, and I grew up around all this. How are you faring so far?"

I instantly like Charlotte. I'm surprised our paths haven't crossed sooner. "I'd say okay, all things considered. I got a crash course in all things royal much sooner than I would have liked."

"Those bloody paparazzi. I can't believe what they did to you. But you've stuck around. That I find quite unbelievable. Not that you would've run, mind you, but most would have." Charlotte steers us to one of the high-top tables. Flowers of all kinds and colours fill the vase on the table.

"Honestly? I'm surprised that didn't send me running to the country." My eyes seek out James. He blends right in with the vets he's chatting with. A smile plays at my lips, one I try to hide. "But James is worth it." I put a little too much force behind my words.

"You don't have to prove it to me, Zara. I can tell."

"You can?" Shock drips from my voice. After those harsh words of the women earlier, it's hard to know.

"Everyone is going to try and tear you down. But believe in what the two of you have. I know how hard this life can be, and finding the right person isn't easy. I'm happy you two found one another. How did the two of you meet? I don't think I've heard the story."

I smirk. "You wouldn't believe me if I told you."

"Charlotte, thanks for keeping Zara company." James had wandered over to us while we were talking.

"Why have you been keeping Zara all to yourself?" Charlotte punches him in the shoulder.

"Because I didn't want you giving her any ideas about how she could do better than me."

Charlotte's laughter is light, as James only stares at her. "Give yourself more credit than that. Half the people here only wish they were as good as you."

I don't miss the shy look on James's face. This wonderful, kind-hearted man does not get enough praise for all he does. He might not have started out doing the best job he could, but it's clear as day on his face how he wants to do a good job, not only for himself, but for his family. His country. I hope for me.

"If you'll excuse us, Charlotte, I was hoping to take Zara on a tour of the palace."

She gives him a side-eye. "Is that what the kids are calling it these days?"

"Piss off." He kisses her cheek before taking my hand in his.

"It was so wonderful to meet you, Charlotte. Maybe we can grab drinks soon?"

Her eyes glimmer with excitement. "That sounds fab. Get my number from James." He's tugging on my arm to move faster. "I don't think a tour is necessarily what he has in mind," she whispers in my ear. Giving her a double cheek kiss, I fall in step behind James. His pace is hurried.

"Where on earth are you taking me?" I jog after him. He pulls me into the gazebo tucked into the private area of the garden. There are no photographers back here.

His lips hungrily seek mine. He tastes like champagne and desire. Of heat and lust. It swirls around us in the warm London air as I open to him. There's a sense of desperation behind this kiss. James likes taking command, and I easily give it to him. He nips at my bottom lip, tugging it between his teeth. There's something in the way he's taking this kiss that sets me on edge.

"Are you alright?" I bemoan the loss of his lips on mine, my voice breathy.

His thumb soothes the sting on my lip. "Just don't like not having you by my side at these kinds of things."

"Nothing's going to happen to me while we're inside

the palace grounds." My heart balloons inside my chest for this man.

"You can't blame me for worrying about you, love." His fingers stroke my cheek, heat sliding through me. I lean into that feeling.

"I'm stronger than you think I am. I can handle it." I say it just as much for him as for myself. I don't tell him that I worry about the paparazzi every time I leave the house. Or that those comments from the women earlier affected me more than I wanted them to. That I hoped I had a smile plastered on my face for the photographers at the event.

"Sometimes I just want you all to myself."

My hands trace the medals decorating his chest. "Think that's something we can make happen sooner rather than later?"

"Anything for you, my queen."

Chapter Nineteen

JAMES

The heat in Zara's eyes has me racing into the palace. I don't mind the royal garden party. I actually enjoy it. Honouring those who have served is always special to me since I served. But with Zara looking exceptionally sexy today in that green dress and fascinator, all I've wanted to do is cut and run as fast as possible. To strip her down and have my way with her.

With hands shaken and stories shared, I lead Zara through the maze of the palace to my office here. My need for her is boiling in my body so high that Egypt feels closer than my office.

Coming upon the right door, I throw it open and pull her inside. She's on me immediately. Her lips capture mine. This kiss is messy. It's passionate. It's everything a kiss should be. My cock gets hard beneath my zipper as her tongue tangles with mine. Running my hands up her thighs, I carry her to my desk, setting her on the edge.

There's a fire in her eyes. Hundreds of people have come out to be recognised by the Queen, and we're up in my office, acting on the desire we both feel for one another.

"I guess once a playboy, always a playboy." Zara's smile is playful as she unbuckles my belt. It's a harsh reminder of why we're in this situation. That situations like this one are precisely why Zara was thrust into my life. But when she slides her dress up her delectable thighs, it's hard to have any thoughts.

Dropping to my knees, I push the fabric of her dress farther up, exposing my end goal. Her thong is wet as her thighs spread open, beckoning me forward.

"Fuck, you're gorgeous." I tongue the wet spot on her lacy thong. Her needy moans tell me she wants more. Brushing the fabric to the side, I suck down on her clit. She's a writhing mess beneath me as I pleasure her with expert strokes of my tongue.

The heels of her shoes are biting into my shoulders. When I thrust two fingers inside of her, she clamps down on me. She's pulsing with need as my cock thickens in my pants. I need to find my own release, but I'm not coming before Zara does.

"Yes! Right there!" Her loud voice carries through the quiet office.

"Fuck, Zara. I need you to come now." I pull my fingers out, thrusting three inside of her. Her hands fist my hair, the spikes of pain mixing with the pleasure I'm driving her towards.

"Oh James!" Her voice is soft as she starts to come. I lap up her release, savouring it on my tongue. It's the sweetest nectar, I think as I drink it in.

When she starts to come down, I stand. Her once pristine hair is messy, and the fascinator lies on the floor behind my desk. When she turns her eyes on me, my heart stops in my chest. The emotions pooling in her eyes cause them to come pouring out of me.

"I love you, Zara. You're the best thing that's ever

happened to me. Fuck, I shouldn't be telling you like this." She pushes up onto her elbows, her skirt still hiked around her waist. She looks utterly defiled. And positively beautiful.

"I know this thing between us was arranged by our parents." I wave a finger between us. "But Christ, I can't help how I feel."

She doesn't say anything. The silence stretches like an ocean between us. I don't think I've misread this situation. The looks. The touches. She has to feel the same way, right? Just when I'm about to go run and hide, a smile cracks her lips. A smile that tells me all I need to know.

"I love you, James." She sits up, wrapping her hands around my neck as she brings me closer to her. "We had the strangest start of anyone I know, but it doesn't make it any less real."

"It's our story." I drop my forehead to hers. My heart could burst from my chest at the love I have for this woman.

"Our story. Think of what we can tell the kids."

I smirk at her. "Kids? Planning ahead now?"

She drops a sweet kiss on the corner of my mouth. "I'm thinking four, at least. Maybe we'll get lucky and have some twins too."

"As long as they all look like you, I'm happy."

A sigh escapes her lips, ghosting my cheek. "As long as they look like you, I'm happy," she parrots my words.

"Maybe we should start practising?" I lean into her, pressing my erection into her centre.

"We'll need all the practise we can get." She stands, giving me her back. I work open my pants, pulling my aching cock out. Pressing her down on the desk, I line myself up with her, before thrusting into heaven. Zara is perfect. This woman is absolutely perfect, and I don't know how I got so lucky to have been given the gift of her.

Zara shakes her arse against me, letting me know to get moving. "Someone's eager, aren't we?" I pull out before slamming back into her. I set an unrelenting pace as she moves underneath me. Her knuckles are white as she clings to the edge of the desk.

"Fuck, you feel incredible." My movements are hurried as I drive into her. Her moans are the only sounds permeating the rush of blood in my head. I lose all coherent thought when I'm around this woman.

"Kiss me." Her voice is breathless, full of need. I wouldn't deny the woman I love anything. I press my weight into her back, seeking her lips with my own. I nibble on her full bottom lip as she starts to come apart around me.

"Don't stop!" Zara screams as her pussy clamps down around me. Heat and desire are coiling at the base of my dick. I'm ready to blow, but I want to draw out Zara's pleasure as long as possible.

Pulling out, I spin Zara around, taking her in my arms. Her legs wrap around my waist as I carry us over to the loveseat. I sit, her on top of me. Finding the zipper in the back of her dress, I inch it down before freeing her breasts. Her nipples are diamond hard as I draw one into my mouth.

"How are you so good at that?" Zara arches into my touch.

"You make it easy, love." I move to her other nipple, as Zara grinds herself over my dick, spreading her wetness around. "But I'm going to need you to fuck me now."

Zara's fingers find my hair, pulling my head back. Staring into my eyes, she lowers herself down. Once she's fully seated, she takes a few settling breaths. I mirror her. It feels good. Too good.

Zara rises, sliding back down, spinning her hips to find her own pleasure. Bloody hell, it feels amazing. She continues to ride me, my own orgasm just out of reach. Her eyes are blazing with fire as she doesn't break contact. Drawing one hand down, I find her clit. Rubbing tight circles around the bundle of nerves, I can tell when she starts to crack. Her movements become more erratic.

I try to fight the heat raging through me, but it erupts from me as she starts to pulse around my dick. I growl as I come, thrusting up into her. Her movements start to still as our orgasms take over. I clutch her to me, needing to stay grounded.

This woman drives me wild in the best way. She makes me feel something I've never felt before. And damn, if I won't spend my entire life trying to make her feel the same.

I slip out of Zara, dropping her on the loveseat at my side. I'm spent. Sated. Happier than I can ever remember being.

"I guess we should return to the party?" Zara pokes my still clothed side. Her breasts are exposed, and her dress is around her waist. My dick is hanging out of my pants. We're quite the picture.

"Like this wouldn't make front page news tomorrow. Future King and Queen naked at current Queen's Garden Party." I throw my hands up, mimicking the news.

"I'd be thrown out on my arse if that were to happen." She says it in jest, but I can't help but grow concerned.

"You know if anything happens, I'll protect you, right?"

She shifts in my arms, looking up at me. "I know." There's doubt in her voice. I don't know why she would think I wouldn't protect her from everything this life brings with it. "It's just hard to predict what they are going to say about us."

I swing her legs over my lap, righting her dress around her before tucking myself back into my pants. This conversation feels too heavy to be doing it partially clothed.

"You have nothing to be worried about. You're the most stand-up person I know. Hell, that's why Mum picked you."

She winces at that statement. "I know, but what if someone were to sneak in here and take pictures of us right now?"

"You know that's not going to happen."

"I know. It's hard to shut off the worry sometimes. I'm not used to this crazy life, and some days it seems really hard."

Is she doubting me? Why would she tell me she loves me if she were going to turn around and dump me? Fuck, this nagging feeling starts tugging at the edges of my brain. I've never been a one-woman kind of man, because I didn't see the point. But with Zara? She's all I can see.

"Hey." Cupping my chin, she turns me to face her. "It's the press I'm worried about. Not you. You and I are solid. Don't doubt us."

Easier said than done.

Chapter Twenty

JAMES

"This is the charity you'd like to set up?" Mum's voice is quiet as she reviews my proposal for her. I'm usually not one to worry about things like this, but for once, I'm taking an active role in my future instead of letting someone hand it to me. I'll be the first to admit I've been acting like a shithead to her these last few weeks, but I was angry.

"Yes. After we took the Smythsons to the football club last week, Zara said it'd be perfect for me. I love sports and children, so why not mix the two? We can help those who are in hospital and set up some programs with local clubs."

Mum stands, rounding her desk to stand in front of me. "This is what I've been looking for from you, darling."

My eyes shoot to hers, confusion no doubt written all over my face. "Really?"

"Yes." Her hands cup my cheeks, a sense of pride emanating from her. "For so long, you did whatever you wanted because you could. And I'm afraid that's partially my fault for focusing so much on your sister. But I wanted you to find something you were passionate about. And this is it."

"You really think so?" I hate that my voice sounds timid and scared. But needing her approval is key to making this happen.

"Run with this, James. I have no doubt you'll see all the success in the world. And I'm so pleased to see Zara helping you with this."

I let out a breath I didn't realize I was holding. "Thanks, Mum." I stand, giving her a hug. It feels pretty damn good having her seal of approval on this.

"I'll always support you, my sweet boy. Sometimes, you just need a good kick in the arse to get there."

I smile at her as I get a shove out the door. I didn't realize how much I needed her validation in this project. So much of what I've done in the past has been because it's been handed to me. But for once, I don't want to do something just because I'm told. I don't want to skate by just because I was born into this life. I want to thrive. My grandfather was perhaps the best King we've had in centuries. I not only want to live up to his legacy, but to surpass him.

Finding my way back to my own office here at the palace, my advisors stand upon my arrival. "We've got some work to do."

"PARDON ME, sir, but if you don't leave now, you'll be late for your dinner with Miss Cross." Charles is at my shoulder. Checking my watch, hours have gone by. With no events on the schedule for today, I took full advantage of working on my new charity. I have so many ideas, and all I can think about is sharing them with Zara.

"Where are we meeting her?" Standing, I slip into my blazer and follow Charles out the door.

"You were going to cook for her tonight." His voice is even as we descend the stairs from my office.

"Did you get takeaway for me?" He gives me a knowing stare as I get into the car.

"Italian is waiting for you at home. Zara will arrive a few minutes after, so it will look like you prepared dinner yourself."

"Excellent." I clap him on the shoulder as we head off. My cooking skills are lacking. As much as I'd like to impress Zara, I don't want to poison her with my nonexistent abilities. Except, I don't think Zara is labouring under the delusion that I know how to cook after Oliver let it slip about my burnt pasta in uni.

Pulling into the grounds in Kensington, my mind eases. It's been a long few days. Things have never been better with Zara. We were off after the wedding was thrown in our faces, but after the Royal Garden Party, we're on the same page. We're connecting more. We easily tell one another how much we love each other. And we definitely show it. I can't get enough of her sexy body. I long for the day when I can wake up to her snuggled up against me.

The paparazzi are eating our every appearance up. I can't remember the last time my picture was on the front page of every tabloid, but there I am. With Zara by my side. I know she hates it, but I love having her there.

The heavy scent of Italian greets me as I walk in the door of the apartment. Heading to my room, I change into something more casual before coming downstairs for a drink.

Eggplant parmesan. Lasagne. Chicken Alfredo. It all

looks delectable. Whoever put this together did a brilliant job.

"James?" Zara's voice carries throughout the house. It's settling. Like she's seeking me out after a long day. That this is something we do on a daily basis. I like that thought more than I should.

Walking out into the formal living room, I find her setting her things down on the back of the couch. "Hi, love."

Her face softens as she looks over at me. The space of the living room separates us. I hate any distance between us.

"You seem to be in a good mood."

"Let's eat and I'll tell you about it."

She nods, walking over to me. Wrapping an arm around her shoulders, I pull her into me. "Where'd you get dinner from?"

"You don't believe I worked all day to make you a feast fit for a queen?" Her hand comes down on my stomach, warming me from the contact.

"If you cooked, we might get food poisoning. And you'd want to make it look like you did, so I'm guessing you had someone get takeout instead of anyone else cooking."

I stop, pulling Zara in front of me. "How the hell could you have guessed that?"

Zara drags her fingers over my cheeks. "I love you, James, and I know you better than you seem to think. Besides, it's what all men do." She walks away, a little more sway in her hips.

"Someone's in a cheeky mood tonight," I whisper, following her into the kitchen.

"It smells delicious." She tucks her hair behind her

back, as she takes a deep inhale of the dishes set out. "Are we eating in here?"

"Good a place as any." She grabs the dishes as she heads for the small table in the corner. I rarely eat in here, but it feels normal with her. I grab some wine for her and settle in beside her.

"So, how was school today? Teach the kids any pop songs?" She cuts into her eggplant, her lips closing around the fork. Fuck, if I don't want to be that fork right now.

"They do like the classics too."

"Do they?" I waggle my eyebrows at her.

"Well, they do when I tell them they have to in order to get the pop songs." She sighs, swirling her wine in her glass. "At least they enjoy playing, so I'll take that most days."

"Kids just don't appreciate the good things in life."

Zara peers at me over her glass. "Oh? And what are those good things in life that you appreciate?"

I reach for her hand, the small rings cold against my skin. "Having a beautiful woman to have dinner with me. Good Italian food. Fine wine."

Her hand flips under mine, holding it in her grip. "What's gotten into you today?" Her fingertips caress my palm. Heat radiates up my arm at the small contact.

"I talked to Mum about the charity idea." Her movements still as she sets her wine glass down. She stands, moving to sit on my lap. Dropping my own fork, I hug her close to me.

"I'm so proud of you. Tell me everything."

The confidence this woman has in me blows me away. It's more than I have in myself some days.

"You really want to hear about it?"

Zara's hands are warm on my face. Emotions swirl in her

eyes—exasperation with a whole lot of love. "Of course I want to hear about it. This is big. I know it can't be easy to tell the Queen you want to blaze your own trail, but you did it."

"I don't deserve you," I blurt out. Fecking hell, this woman is ruining me. Dropping my head to her shoulder, I try to calm my now racing heart. Zara is one of the most beautiful people I have ever met. Not just on the outside, but the inside too. I've never met anyone who loves their job like she does. She has such a passion for what she does, and a love for those around her, that it's hard not to want to be around her.

"That's just not true. Look at me." Her fingers under my chin bring my gaze to hers. Her eyes are soft. "There is a heart of gold under all this bravado. You don't want people to see the real you, because you don't want to be rejected."

"Coming with the big guns," I say on a laugh, trying to diffuse the tension of the moment.

"Stop it." This time, her fingers grab my chin, holding my focus to her. "If you didn't care, you wouldn't have taken the Smythsons to Chelsea. You wouldn't have gone above and beyond for them. If you didn't care, we wouldn't be here. You would've said fuck it and renounced the crown like your sister."

It's a staggering thought. Would I have given this all up if I didn't care? Would I have lived life in the fast lane until I ran out of gas?

"You are showing up whether you want to believe it or not. You are going to do amazing things as the prince and future King. Don't doubt yourself."

"You make it sound so easy."

"If there's one thing I've learned these last few weeks," her voice comes out soft, "is that none of this is easy. You learn to deal with the hard as it comes, and you get better at it."

"And are you getting better at dealing with the hard?" Zara had the worst crash course with the paparazzi, and it's difficult not to worry about her anytime she's out on her own.

She doesn't answer right away, causing my heart rate to increase. I keep waiting for the other shoe to drop. For her to decide that this life I lead isn't worth it. That I'm not worth it.

"Some days it feels easy. Some days it's hard. Really hard. Like I worry about what would happen if the paparazzi got into school or did something to one of my students."

Fuck. I never thought about that. About what could happen if someone crossed the line. It's not just Zara I need to worry about.

"But the security officers help. Being around you helps. I know people in the past have used you for leverage to increase their station in life, or a quick screw with the prince, but that's not me." Her eyes are gentle as she drops her forehead to mine. "I want you to know you're worth all this craziness, James. Even on the days I doubt myself, I never have any doubts about you. Or us. I love you more than I thought possible."

My heart swells in my chest. No one has ever said that. Like Zara said, they either want to sleep with the prince or try to get ahead in life. But Zara has never been that person. And it's taken meeting her to realize that I don't have a lot of people like her in my life. Most people are passing acquaintances. I have a tight-knit circle, but it's remained small because I haven't found anyone worth bringing into the fold.

But Zara is worth it. I love her so much, it hurts some-

times. Even if we met under the strangest of circum-
stances, I know I'll do everything in my power to keep her
safe. Even if it means keeping her safe from me. I never
want to dull this light that she has.

There are no words that can be said, so I simply wrap
her in my arms. This beautiful, perfect, amazing woman
that I am not worthy of. Zara may not have her doubts
about us, but right now, in this moment, I'm full of them.
Wondering if there is any future between the two of us
that doesn't end in heartbreak.

Chapter Twenty-One

ZARA

"Alright, everyone. Sit up straight and instruments at the ready." Snickers break out across the room. "Okay, okay. Let's go."

From the moment they first sat down, they've been antsy. Whispering amongst themselves throughout class. If they weren't playing so well, it'd be more grating. Thankfully, it's the last class of the day.

Tapping my baton, the music starts to rise, and the practice of this week is noticeable. It's coming together and not a moment too soon, with the end of term recital coming up in the next week.

As the song starts to crescendo, the headmaster of the school makes his way into the back of the classroom. His face is drawn tight in dismay as he looks at his watch and then me. Nerves settle deep in my stomach. What in the world is he doing in here? Outside of formal evaluations, it's rare to see him in our classrooms. And considering we have them once a year, and mine was at the start of the term, his presence is unnerving.

We work through the piece a few more times before it's

time to pack up for the day. A few students are lingering before they're dismissed by the headmaster. They shoot curious glances back at me as he closes the door behind the last student.

"Miss Cross. I need a word with you."

Ice settles in my stomach at his tone. "Okay." I sit at my desk, taking in his discerning stare.

"Effective immediately, you are suspended for conduct detrimental to the terms of the contract you signed upon hire."

"What?" I explode out of my seat. "What conduct are you referring to?"

He slaps a magazine on the desk in front of me, and all blood seems to drain from my body. My stomach is somewhere near my feet as I read the headlines.

Our future Queen riding the Prince too hard?

BELOW THE HEADLINE is a picture of my first night with James. I'm on top of him as our naked bodies are exposed. "I don't understand. How did they get this?"

"There's more," he says, taking the magazine from my hands and flipping it open. There are more pictures from that night. The night that James took me to the orchestra. The same night I realized I was falling in love with him.

His words are distant as the pictures in front of me assault my eyes. Of James's hands all over me. Of his kisses. Of me stroking him off. Every single moment from that evening is plastered all over this gossip rag for the world to see.

"As you can see, these are rather disturbing. And this

goes against the contract you signed when you started here."

"This is an invasion of privacy!"

"And yet I can't ignore these images. I've already had several calls from parents concerned about the level of scrutiny these photos will bring down on the school. Until this dies down, we can't have you teaching."

I can only shake my head in dismay. Grabbing my purse, I leave the room without another word.

"Miss Cross. Please wait until we can have the car brought around." My security officer stops me at the side door.

"Is it bad?"

He pins me with a look that tells me it is. "Prince James is awaiting your arrival."

I nod as the door is pushed open and a wall of sound hits me. Flashbulbs are popping in my face as I'm guided out of the school. Bodies are pushing on all sides of me. It's worse than when they attacked me outside my house. They're screaming at me left and right.

"Is this how you plan to run the country?"

"Did you only want James because he's going to be King?"

"Are you just doing this for the attention?"

"How is the prince in bed?"

Bile is thick in my throat as I make my way into the awaiting car. Tears threaten as I pull out my phone. Hundreds of notifications are awaiting me, but I ignore them all. I know I shouldn't look at the damage, but I have to see what is being said.

I don't have to search hard. The images are at the top of every major news headline. At least some have the decency to blur out some of the more risqué photos.

Most of the photos are from that night at the orchestra

with James. But there are a few others. Us in my garden one night. Laughing in the kitchen. They're tame. I'm sitting on his lap while we had drinks. Nothing devastating like the ones of us having sex in my room.

I can't figure out how they took those photos. I'm in a quiet neighbourhood, surrounded by houses on all sides. Aside from misplaced post, my neighbours are quiet and keep to themselves. Who in their right mind would do something like this?

A fierce ache settles in my bones. I knew it wouldn't be an easy life, stepping into the royal spotlight. But I never thought my life would be invaded in such a drastic manner. The fact that my privacy was violated in such an epic fashion, in my own home no less, has doubts about this new life swirling in my head.

Will it always be like this?

Will they be able to protect us from the press?

How far will they go to get a story?

Kensington is swarming with press as we pull through the gates. Never in my life have I seen so many people crowded into such a tiny area, all hoping to get the money shot of the disgraced prince and his girlfriend. Is this really what I have to look forward to now that James and I are together? It's a sickening thought as we pull up to his apartment. He's outside waiting for me.

James eats up the distance between us as soon as the door is open.

"Zara. I'm so sorry this happened." He pulls me into his arms, his heart thundering in his chest.

"Let's talk inside." His brows are furrowed, and distress mars his handsome features.

Shutting the door behind us, the scent of James overwhelms me. Tears prickle the back of my eyes as I take in his distressed stance.

"How did this happen?" My voice is quiet as we move into his living room. "How could someone release photos like that?"

"They don't care about the damage they do. Only that they hit us where it hurts most."

"Well, they've certainly done that," I say on a huff.

"It will all blow over, I promise. This has happened to me before, and it'll leave the news cycle in a few weeks."

"A few weeks? I was suspended from school today because it's detrimental to the students I'm teaching!" I shriek. "I'm sorry I can't brush it off as easily as you, but our sex life is out there for everyone to see!"

James winces as he starts pacing again. "I didn't mean for you to brush it off. It's just this sort of thing will always be a threat as a royal."

"You mean I should always be worried that we'll be photographed having sex and it'll be released for the world to see?" I hit him with my most indignant glare.

"No, I don't mean that, Z." He approaches me, but I pull away. "Zara, love. Please, sit down and I'll tell you how I'm handling this."

I turn, settling my hands on my hips. "And how are you handling this?" I'm in no mood to be told what to do.

"You don't need to be so defensive."

"Oh, I'm sorry. You're right. No big deal that my tits are out there for the entire world to see!"

Walking over to the window, I see that clouds are starting to move into the city, much like my mood.

"Zara. I'm sorry. We have people looking into this. I don't know how the pictures were taken, but the palace will certainly get to the bottom of it."

"And how do you plan on preventing this from happening again?" I don't turn to face him. Dread hangs heavy in the air.

Dread that this can happen again.

Dread that I won't be able to recover from this.

Dread that my life has been altered beyond recognition.

"We'll just have to be more careful next time." James's hands wrap around my waist, pulling me into him.

"Weren't we being careful the first time?" I twist out of his hold. His arms, that are always so calming, only cause tremors to wrack my body.

"Zara, please. We'll get through this."

"Will we?" My voice cracks. I don't know how I'm going to be able to handle this. Or anything like this in the future.

"It's one scandal."

"This week. What about next week? Or next month? Or next year? What if I can't handle it? The paparazzi follow me everywhere. I'm already losing so much."

"What are you saying?" Pain is evident in his eyes.

"I just don't know if I can do this, James."

He sinks down onto the sofa, holding his head in his hands. He looks so despondent sitting there as the world weighs me down.

"You knew that this would be part of the risk of getting involved with me." James's voice is hollow. I've never heard such emptiness come from such a happy person.

"Maybe I didn't have the full picture. I never expected to have the paparazzi attack me outside my own home or invade my privacy inside my home." My hand goes to the healed cut on my cheek. "I just, I don't know if I can handle this life."

James shoots up and crosses to me in a quick stride. "Please don't say that, Zara. We love each other. We can work through this."

His hands are warm on my cheeks as the tears finally

fall, carving hot paths down my face. "What if we can't? What if it only gets worse?"

"All I can do is promise to protect you with everything I have. I don't want to lose you."

The guilt in his eyes is crushing. "I'm sorry, James. I just need time."

"How much time?" The crack in his voice splits my heart in two.

"I don't know." Grasping his hands, I kiss his knuckles before stepping out of his hold.

"That's not reassuring, love."

"I'm sorry, I'm not sure what else I can do right now." James's presence is overwhelming. So much so, I can't stand to be here a moment longer. Rushing to grab my bag, I try to leave as fast as possible.

"That's it? You're just leaving me here without another word?"

The break in my heart is too much. The tears tracking down my face are endless. "I told you I need time."

"Bullshit. You're running scared. Time is never a good thing, and you'll find every excuse to not be with me because you're not ready for everything this world is."

"Can you blame me? I'm sorry, but after today, I don't think I'm asking for too much."

"Well, it's too much for me. Because if you walk through that door, we're done."

The finality of his tone hits me square in the chest. "Fine. If that's how you want this to go, then we're done." Just saying those words causes another crack in my heart.

"Then I guess we are." Opening the door, my security officer offers me an umbrella in the now rainy skies. It matches my own misery. I run through the rain to the awaiting car. I'll no longer have the security officers to protect me from the paparazzi. My life is a pendulum, going from complete anonymity to being in the public spotlight with James, to losing the sense of comfort I have with him and being thrown to the wolves on my own.

And as we pull away, the palace grounds getting farther and farther behind us, the ache in my heart deepens. I wanted time. James couldn't possibly expect me to bounce back after an hour, could he?

But now, now I don't even have the option of bouncing back. Because he was swift to cut me out of his life. Just like all the bimbos he's ever been with. I really did fall for the playboy prince.

Chapter Twenty-Two

JAMES

The pounding in my head is getting louder. Bloody hell, why won't it go away? Sitting up, I realize it's coming from my front door. Just what I want, to be around people right now.

The sun is blinding as I get off the sofa. The room spins ever so slightly. I yank open the front door, and my mum, my grandmum, and Ellie greet me. "Oh goodie. Just who I wanted to see right now." I stalk back to the living room, not bothering to wait for them to come in.

"James, we need to discuss what happened." Mum's voice is firm as she takes a seat across from me.

"What's there to discuss? Someone took photos of Zara and me having sex and leaked them to the press." I'm wallowing, and I know it. "Zara was the best thing to ever happen to me, and now she's gone."

"Is she though?" Ellie's voice is hard as she shoves me from the side. "Have you talked to her?"

I collapse back onto the sofa, my head resting in my grandmum's lap. It's like I'm five years old again. "She wanted time, but you know what that means."

"Perhaps that she needed time to wrap her head around this?" Grandmum has always been straightforward. "I never had to worry about my naughty bits being strewn across the news for the world to see."

I huff out a laugh. "Thank God for that!"

She pinches my side. "I didn't ask for your cheek, darling. Why did you push her away?"

Why did I push her away? "Because I was scared. I was scared she was going to run and be just like everyone else who used me for my title."

"That's a load of crap and you know it. Anyone who saw the two of you together knows how in love you were." Ellie smacks me on the arm.

I rub my hands down my face. My beard is getting scraggly. I haven't left the house since Zara walked out on me. I didn't want the paparazzi to get a shot of the haggard-looking prince.

I shift my gaze to Mum. "I was trying. I was really trying to be better." My voice breaks.

"Oh darling." Mum walks over, crouching down to face me. "You don't have to be better. You just have to be you."

"Isn't being me what got us into this mess to start with?"

Her hand is warm on my cheek. "No. You had it in you this whole time. You just needed someone to see it in you."

Zara was that person. She saw me for me. I wasn't just someone with a title to sleep with. I wasn't just a prince to her. I was just James. Why couldn't I see that?

"How am I going to get her back?"

"Well for starters, you might want to shower and shave." Grandmum tugs at my beard. "No offence, but the beard isn't a great look for you."

I laugh. "Thanks, Grandmum."

"I'm not going to make it easy for you." She lifts me off

her lap, my eyes tearing up at some of the most important people in my life surrounding me at one of my lowest moments.

"Have you thought about what you want to do with your charity?" Mum starts cleaning up the empty bottles from the table.

"I have a general idea of what I want to do. Why?"

Mum shifts her gaze to Ellie. "Has he always been this clueless?"

Ellie laughs, shaking her head at me. "Of course. He's a man." Her hand is mindlessly rubbing her baby bump.

"I really hope you have a girl," I tease.

"James. Move up the kick-off of the event. Don't let the press beat you down. Instead of rebounding by going to the clubs—"

I cut her off. "I haven't been to the clubs in ages. It's never even crossed my mind."

"Aww, my baby brother is finally growing up after twenty-nine years."

"Piss off," I say on a laugh. I give her a weak smile.

"You may be down, but you're not out. Counter this scandal with starting your charity. People will see the good in you, and it'll become this wonderful thing."

I pull Ellie in for a hug. I've clearly had too much to drink, because I'm more emotional than I usually am. "You're going to make a great mum, Ellie."

Her eyes are wet when she pulls back. "Okay. Plan of attack. Throw a huge gala and invite Zara."

"Just need to plan a whole gala in only a few weeks?"

"Oh, however will you manage?" Mum comes back into the room. "Whatever you need, whoever you need to help you, they are at your disposal. Perks of the crown." She smirks at me.

"I better get started then."

"Fab. Do you have a name for this new charity you are starting?" Ellie asks.

"Sporting Kids?" I blurt out. It's the first thing that comes to mind.

"Sporting Kids? Are you set on that?" Ellie turns her nose up at the name.

"You really going to kick a man when he's down?"

"Not what I would've picked, but have at it. I need to get to the school. Let me know if you need help." Ellie drops a kiss on my head before leaving.

"Thanks, El." She winks on her way out the door.

"I think we've got you all sorted out." Grandmum stands, following Ellie. "Just make sure to close the curtains next time."

"Grandmum, I don't need you telling me that."

"How do you think your granddad and I kept it under wraps all those years?"

"Mum!" Mum's voice carries over the room.

"I'm scarred for life." If a hole would open up and swallow me down, I'd be forever grateful right about now.

"Katherine, are you joining me?"

"Give me a minute." Grandmum heads outside, leaving me with Mum.

"Are you going to be alright?" Mum's voice is quiet as she sits next to me.

My happiness shouldn't be so dependent on one person, but I can't help it. I've never met anyone like Zara.

"I'm sorry for all the trouble I've been lately. I know I haven't been easy on you these last few weeks, and I'm sorry."

"I'm the one who should be sorry. I didn't have enough faith that you could make a name for yourself. I was so worried that you would renounce your place in line to the throne like Ellie that I held on too hard."

Tears linger in her eyes. What is in the air today that is making everyone so emotional? "If it wasn't for you, I wouldn't have met Zara. I hated the idea of you finding my wife, but now I can't imagine my life without her."

Mum takes my hand. "Then tell her that. Tell her how much she means to you. Don't lose your chance at a once in a lifetime love over something that won't mean anything in a few weeks' time."

I stand, giving Mum a crushing hug. "I think that's the best idea you've had in a long time."

Chapter Twenty-Three

ZARA

"Zara! Are you home?" Dad's voice echoes throughout the living room. I've sequestered myself here the last few days, curtains drawn, so no one can see me.

"Hi Dad." I peer up from my spot on the sofa as he shuffles into the room.

"Why in the bloody hell are you moping about like this? I thought you'd be happy."

I shoot up as he sits next to me. "Happy? Why in the world would I be happy about any of this?"

"I figured with the paparazzi getting ahold of those photos, you'd be let out of your arrangement."

I give him a puzzled look. "Why would I be let out of it?"

"Because you never wanted it in the first place."

On top of everything else, I'm a terrible daughter. I was so wrapped up in my anger at my father that when things became serious with James, I didn't tell him. Tears burst from my eyes. I can't stop them. They're uncontrollable, as Dad pulls me into a hug. Deep sobs escape as I try to get them under control.

"I fell in love with him." My voice shakes, and my dad squeezes me tighter. "Not only was I a terrible daughter for ignoring your calls because I was upset with you, but I also fell in love with the prince and didn't bother to tell you."

"My darling girl." He pulls back, wiping the tears from my eyes. "You remind me so much of your mum. She could stay mad at me for days. No matter how much I buttered up to her, she'd freeze me out."

My tears lessen at the mention of Mum. "Apparently I learned that from her."

"You learned quite a lot from her. She was the most talented violinist I'd ever heard until you came along. It's like a piece of her is still with me whenever I hear you play."

"I hate that her violin was destroyed. I guess I don't have to worry about the paparazzi doing that again."

"Do you love him?" His brows furrow together, as if it's the worst thing in the world for his little girl to fall in love.

"Yes,"—I bite down on my lip, trying to stop the quiver—"with all my heart."

"As much as I hate that I drew you into my mess, I can't say that I'm too upset that you found the person you wanted to spend your life with."

I pull back, piercing him with a fiery look. "Why did you agree to this arrangement in the first place?"

A harsh look crosses his face. "For the money."

I roll my eyes. "I should've known. But if you were hard for money, why didn't you come to me?" It's not like I make millions teaching, but I would never want my dad to be out on the street.

"It's embarrassing. Being in debt and having no way out. And when the Queen came to me, I thought it would be the perfect solution. But I just hate the pain I've caused you."

I throw my arms around him. "I'm only in pain because I fell in love. So as upset as I want to be with you, I just wish there was a way to get him back."

Just as he's about to respond, a knock at the door stops him. "Aren't they supposed to stay back on the other side of the street? Don't you still have protection officers?"

I just shrug my shoulders as Dad goes to get the door. My protection detail hadn't disappeared like I thought it would. It was some comfort that I wasn't totally on my own with the madness of the paparazzi. But I still only felt safe in my own home.

"Your Highness. It's a pleasure to meet you." My heart clutches in my chest. But why would Dad say it's a pleasure to meet James? They've met before. A belly precedes the former princess into my living room. A short, black dress swings around her knees, clinging to her adorable baby bump. Her appearance is striking. Long pink hair and bright blue eyes. So similar to James it makes my heart ache.

"Ellie? What are you doing here?"

"I was hoping to have a word with you about my brother. May I?" She points to the chair next to me, and I nod for her to sit. "Thanks. This baby is really starting to wear me out."

"I'll let you two ladies talk. Call me if you need me." Dad drops a kiss on my head and heads to the door.

"I love you, Dad." He gives me a smile before the noise outside briefly permeates my bubble of safety. I turn my attention back to Ellie, feeling just a tad better.

"How much longer?" Her hands are resting on her bump. She's glowing.

"About three months. And it can't come soon enough. I'm ready to meet this little one."

"And you still haven't found out what you're having?" I

want to keep her talking about anything other than James. I need to know how he's doing, but I also don't want to hear that he's moved on without me. I've been doing my best not to check the news about him. The only thing that comes up is if we've had sex in a new place. But I want to see if he's doing okay.

"It's one of the last few surprises in life. Sean is dying to find out, but as long as he or she is healthy, I'm happy. But I didn't come here to talk about my baby, as much as I love to. Why are you still here and not at the palace with Jamie?"

My face twists in confusion. "What do you mean, why am I not at the palace? I'm assuming you spoke with James. He couldn't give me the time I needed to come to terms with everything that happened, so he said we were done."

I draw my quivering lip between my teeth. I don't want to cry in front of Ellie. I've done enough of that this week.

"But why did you need time? Why didn't you rely on James to help you come to terms with what happened?"

I must look like a fish, opening and closing my mouth, but no words come out. It's a harsh statement, but one I needed to hear. Why didn't I rely on James? It's not as if he hasn't faced his own scandals in the past. Did I cut and run because it would be easier than facing a life in the press?

"Look, I am not the role model in how to handle the paparazzi. But Jamie needs someone to be there when the going gets tough. If you can't handle it, you need to make a clean break of it now."

"James already made a clean break of it." My heart sinks at the thought. Just the mere idea of an arranged marriage with the "playboy prince" had me balking. But now? Now, it's hard to imagine my life without him.

"Would I be here if he did? He's a sodding mess.

Cancelled every event until the fundraiser event for his new charity. Sporting Kids, I think?"

My eyes shoot up to hers. "He named it?" My heart falls to my feet. He was so excited about this idea. It was his passion project. And I wasn't there for this. "But Sporting Kids? Really?"

Ellie turns her nose up. "Definitely not his best work, but he's not functioning properly."

"Is anyone going to be there for him?" It's not my place anymore, but my mind goes to supporting him. Even if we're not together anymore.

"You are. I don't go to any events where the press is, and it's you he wants by his side."

Tears blur my vision. "He really wants me there?"

Ellie stands, moving to sit next to me. Taking my hands in hers, she brings them to her lap. "He didn't explicitly say it, but I can tell. It's a twin thing."

I give her a sad smile. "Will he even take me back?"

Her grip is firm as I look into her clear, blue eyes. "Show him he's worth it. Every person up until this point in his life has only wanted to be with him because he's the prince. You didn't stay. He thinks that he's not worth it."

I shoot up out of her grasp. "But he is! He's the most wonderful person I've ever met in my life, and I can't imagine not being with him. He's never been the 'playboy prince' to me. He's James, the soft, caring man who will be the best King this nation has ever seen."

Ellie's face is warm as she looks up at me. "And you'll be the perfect Queen by his side."

"Am I able to attend the event for his charity?" There's no way I can miss this.

Ellie pulls a card from her bag. "Here's all the details. I've talked to Charlotte, and she'll send someone over to help you out with a dress and your hair this week. A car will pick you up, so you don't have to worry about getting there."

"I appreciate all that, but I think I can take care of my dress and hair."

And I have just the outfit that will hopefully bring James to his knees. And hopefully bring us back together.

Chapter Twenty-Four

JAMES

There are hundreds of people in this room, and I've never felt more alone. Sure, a few friends are lingering here and there, but there's no one at my side.

The dull ache in my heart roars to full strength. Tonight will be a good night. The official start of Sporting Kids. My very first, and my very own, charity. And the one person I want by my side isn't here.

"Things seem to be going well. There are a few more donors we'd like you to speak with before your presentation." Charles has been at my shoulder all night, reminding me of everything that needed to be done. Typically, the royals wouldn't be in charge of fundraising, but with this being my passion project, I wanted to be involved in every aspect.

"Start with Lord Browning. I hear he's wanting to diversify his charity holdings this year."

I nod, sipping on the champagne in my hand. It's an open bar, but I don't want to get pissed like I have been for the last few weeks. As I start making my way to the lord in question, whispers break out across the room. Can't I just go one night without some scandal?

"Your Highness. I would suggest heading to the press area. Miss Cross is here, and we don't want anything to happen tonight."

Zara's here? But how in the world did she know about this? The charity was only in the beginning stages when I talked to her last. Cutting a path through the crowds, my beautiful Zara is making her way into the room. The click of cameras is louder than anything else in the room.

Zara is wearing the dress. The same red dress she wore to the orchestra that night that hugs every curve and dip of her sexy body. Her long, dark waves fall around her shoulders. She's a life raft for someone who has been drowning in his own misery these last few weeks.

We invited the press tonight to help boost the visibility of the charity. Not that it wouldn't get out on its own, but I wanted the work we're doing to be covered here tonight as well.

"Zara! Where have you been hiding since the scandal broke?"

"Zara! Is it true you're addicted to sex?"

"Care to give your side of the scandal?"

Oh, for fuck's sake. Handing my glass to Charles, I head to Zara's side. She's stiff. She's not the easygoing Zara that I'm used to.

"Thank you all for coming. I appreciate you being here, but I need Miss Cross." I go to pull Zara away from the press, but her hand on my bicep has me stopping. Her eyes are clear. She gives me a small nod and turns to the press.

"Thank you all for being here to show your support for Prince James and his new charity, Sporting Kids." Zara's lips quirk up in the barest hint of a smile. Damn, she's giving me grief over the name too. Really not my best work.

"As for a statement, I will give one, and one only." Her fingers tighten on my arm, and I cover her hand with mine. "What was leaked to the press was a private moment between two people in love. It was a violation of our privacy, and the person who took those photos was trespassing on private property."

She turns to me, her eyes steely as I can see she's gearing up. "It was inappropriate for them to be released, and they should not have been cycled through the news. I hope more care is taken to spreading the good work that James is doing here tonight, and not illegally taken photos of us. Our focus will always be on the work we can do to better our country and our people, and not our private lives."

Damn. I don't think I've ever heard anyone put the press in their place better than that. The royal family is not one to give statements based on rumours or gossip they spread, but I know how hard it was on Zara being thrust into the spotlight. And this was her taking back control. My future Queen. I'm bursting with pride at the woman before me.

"Zara. What role will you play in the new charity?" She turns to me, her eyes now sparkling.

"That's up to the prince to decide."

"James?" A microphone is thrust my way.

I don't see who is talking to me. My sole focus is on Zara and that she's here tonight. That she stood up to the press, for herself. For both of us. That has to mean something, right?

"She'll have whatever role she wants. Now, if you'll excuse us." I take her warm hand in mine, leading her away from the press.

"What are you doing here?" I whisper, grabbing a glass of champagne for her from a passing waiter.

"I was told you might need some support tonight."

My heart swells. She came here for me. I don't want to read too much into it, but it's hard not to. "Fuck, it's good to see you, Zara." The words burst out before I can stop them.

She pulls on my arm, leading me away from the crowds. "We have a lot to discuss. Maybe I can come over tonight so we can talk?" Her voice is small.

"It's going to be a long night."

She shakes her head. "I don't care. I don't have anywhere to be tomorrow."

I wince. I know she was suspended from school, and I hate that. "Yes. I'll wait up all night if it means I can talk to you."

"Excuse me, Your Highness. But I was hoping I could have a word with you?" A tap on my shoulder breaks the moment between me and Zara.

"A prince's work is never done." She gives me a bright smile, telling me she's okay with me being pulled away.

"Save me a dance later?"

"I'll dance with no one but you."

Clutching my hand to my heart, I follow the man who wanted to talk to me, counting down the minutes until I can have Zara in my arms.

Zara

"Now before we turn you all loose for the rest of the evening, Prince James would like to say a few words."

My nerves have been getting the better of me all night. Sidelong glances from people here tell me they've all seen the pictures of us. I hate that a private moment between us was splashed across the news for the world to see.

But after talking with Ellie, I accepted it's part of this life. One that I knew I'd have to come to terms with if it meant keeping James. So I came here tonight, armed with a confidence I don't fully feel, and said my piece. The awe in James's eyes was worth it.

"Good evening." James clears his voice, looking out amongst the crowded room. His eyes settle on me. He takes a deep breath and turns back to the audience.

"I'm incredibly thankful that all of you came out here tonight to help launch Sporting Kids." Claps break through his speech. "It's been an interesting few months for us royals. I never thought I'd be the one to ascend the throne after my mum, and I'm sure not many of you thought that either."

People laugh at his self-deprecation. I only wince, knowing how those words ate away at him.

"It's the honour of a lifetime to serve this wonderful country. And in doing so, I wanted to follow my own passions in life. And that led me to Sporting Kids. After a visit to the new hospital wing in my grandfather's memory, I met the Smythson family, who were kind enough to join us this evening." They have a seat of honour at the table in front of the stage.

"As a child, it's hard being in hospital, and I wanted to make that easier for George. When his love of sport came to light, it gave me the idea for this charity. For children who are sick or are suffering, I want to give them the gift of sport. By working with national and local teams, we are hoping to have this program off the ground and throughout the country by next year. Because keeping kids' spirits up through the love of the game is something we can all agree on. Thank you."

Tears leak out of my eyes at James's beautiful words. His eyes find mine as he hops off the stage, giving George a high five. This incredible, wonderful, kind-hearted man. Why did I ever think I needed time from him?

James is pulled in different directions as people talk and ask him questions about the charity. The band starts to play as people head onto the dance floor.

"Lady Zara, may I have this dance?" Lord Paxton, the older man from the museum charity, is at my side. Pasting on my best smile, I accept his proffered arm.

"It would be a pleasure."

He guides me out onto the dance floor as couples spin and float around us.

"And how are you doing this fine evening, Lord Paxton?" My voice is sugary sweet. This man's ego loves to be inflated. "Did your lovely wife join you this evening?"

"She did. I believe she is off talking to some of the young footballers." Sounds about right.

"It was quite nice for James to have the support of the local London teams." James's eyes track mine, finding me across the dance floor. He excuses himself as he makes his way towards me.

"And your support. I thought you'd hide away after the scandal, but stiff upper lip and all. I'm pleased to see you two weathering the storm together."

"That's very kind of you to say." And I mean it. Instead of him leering at me like he did at the museum and like others have tonight, his show of support means more than I can say. An ally in a group of people who will become my peers.

"And you should know that James has my support with Sporting Kids. However I can help. I hope for nothing but the best for you both."

"Thank you. We truly appreciate your support. And now if you don't mind, I think there's someone who would like to cut in." He turns to see James waiting patiently with his hands tucked into his pockets.

"Ahh. We shall not keep the prince waiting any longer. Your Highness." He dips into a bow as he kisses my hand.

"It was a pleasure, Lord Paxton." James steps in, his hand on me a comfort I've missed these last few weeks.

"I see you've taken quite easily to the schmoozing portion of the evening."

I give his hand a squeeze, tucking my chin on his shoulder. I love how evenly matched we are. "It's easy to sell schmooze when you believe in something wholeheartedly. You are going to do amazing things with Sporting Kids."

"Tell me the truth. You hate the name?" His laugh is hot on my cheek. It reverberates through my body.

"Is there still time to change it?"

"Guess I shouldn't make big life decisions when I'm bloody well pissed then, eh?"

My heart hurts at the thought. "And why were you drinking so much?"

James's warm hand slides up my back between my bare shoulders. Heat radiates from his touch. I've missed his touch. The way his face lights up when he sees me.

"Christ, I've missed you, Zara. Letting you walk out of my house was the worst mistake I've ever made."

"James, I—"

"Your Highness, we have a donor that would like to speak with you." Charles appears out of thin air at our side. James lets out a deep breath.

"To be continued?" he asks, his face lined with sadness.

"I'll meet you at your place later." Kissing my knuckles, he walks away.

This time, when he walks away, I don't worry it's going to be the last time. We didn't have the most normal start to our relationship. Most people meet and decide to date before wanting to get married. I was so against this whole arranged marriage, but now I can't imagine my life without James. And all I want is a future with him.

Chapter Twenty-Five

JAMES

It's late, after one in the morning. The kickoff event for Sporting Kids went better than I ever could have imagined. We raised more money than I thought possible, and the icing on the cake? Zara was there. I had no idea what it meant, but it was more than I could have hoped for.

A soft knock at the door has my palms sweating. A brick of nerves settles heavy in my stomach. I don't know what's going to happen, but Zara showing up tonight had to be a good thing, right?

"Zara." I open the door. Her long legs are bare beneath her trench coat. Her stride is purposeful as she walks by me into the living room. "Can I take your coat? Get you a drink?"

"Gin and tonic, please."

Mixing Zara her drink, I sit on the sofa. She's standing before me, finishing her drink in two gulps. Our combined nerves hang heavy in the air.

"Zara—"

She cuts me off. "Me first."

She comes and stands in front of me, running her

hands through my hair. Christ, that feels good. "I'm sorry I panicked after everything that happened. Nothing like that has ever happened to me before, and I didn't know what to do."

"And I'm sorry I didn't prepare you for something like that."

Her fingers cover my lips. "How could you have known something like that would've gotten out? It was such a violation of my privacy that I didn't know what to do. But I shouldn't have run away."

"But you weren't running away." My words are muffled against her hand.

"I was, I just didn't realize it at the time. But Ellie helped me see that instead of running, I should have leaned on you."

I'm shocked. "Ellie talked to you?" When they came to see me, I never thought she'd seek out Zara.

She nods. "You've been through this before. You know how to handle the press. And I ran scared instead of coming to you. No amount of time could ever get me prepared to handle the paparazzi." Her lips start to quiver. "By running, I was like every other woman who just wanted you for your name only."

"Zara, no. Absolutely not." Gripping her hips, I pull her between my legs. "Having your privacy violated like that isn't something anyone should have to worry about." I rest my head on her belly. "If it helps, we caught the guy. He paid off your neighbours to sneak onto their roof to take pictures."

She shakes her head. "I guess it's going to be hard to know who to trust in this life."

"Yes." I look up into her eyes. I don't want to lie to her. "It's going to be hard, and you'll stumble and make mistakes along the way. But I'll be there to help you. Right by your side, where I should've been to start with."

"I still don't think I'm prepared for this role, but I know you'll help me."

My breath catches. "Are you saying what I think you're saying?"

She smiles, her eyes shining with tears. "James, when our parents told us we were to be married, I never thought I'd fall in love with you. But I have. And there's no one else I want in this world. I know what it comes with. As long as we're together, we can weather any storm."

"Fuck, Zara." I drop my head to her stomach, pulling her close to me. Her hands are holding me there. For the first time in weeks, I can breathe easy. "I love you so damn much. These last few weeks have been bloody awful without you."

"Who would've thought that the two of us would've ended up here?" she asks.

Her fingers find my chin, tilting it upward. "Only us." She dips her head down, giving me a soft kiss. Fuck, I never thought I'd get to feel these lips again. I run my tongue along the seam of her lips, and she opens. Her gin-soaked lips are bliss. The velvety softness of her tongue has my cock hardening behind my joggers.

Pulling her onto my lap, my hands drift up her legs. The higher my hands go, the less material they encounter.

"Zara, love?"

"Yes?" I can feel her smiling against my lips.

"Are you wearing anything under this coat?"

"Why don't you find out?" She sits back on my thighs, the belt of her coat drawing my attention. Untying it, the sides fall loose at her side. A small swath of fabric covering her beautiful pussy is the only thing she's wearing. Her tits and hard nipples are on display for me.

"Fuck me."

"That's the point."

Slipping her arms out of the coat, I lift her into my arms, carrying her up the stairs to my room. Her lips are trailing a hot path up and down my neck. I'm ready to combust if I don't get her under me.

Throwing her on the bed, I slip out of my T-shirt and sweats. My dick is tenting my briefs. I crawl towards her on the bed, her heated gaze drawing me in. My world revolves around this woman. She's the sun, and I'm helpless to do anything but spin around her.

"Are you just going to stare at me, or are you going to fuck me?"

"Are you trying to kill me?" My voice is filled with heat and need.

Kissing my way up her legs, I rip that tiny excuse for underwear off her in one pull.

"Gah!" Her pussy is glistening with need as I swipe a finger through her folds. Zara arches into my touch. Goose pimples break out on her skin as I lower my lips to her clit. Pressing her legs wide, I lavish attention on her pussy. Licking and sucking on the tight bundle of nerves, I press two fingers into Zara's tight channel. Her walls are already pulsing with need.

"That feels incredible." Zara's voice is greedy as her hands grip my hair. The sting of pleasure has me finding friction on the bed. I can't wait to be in her tight heat. "I'm so close."

Pulling off her, I leave her riding the edge of orgasm. "I want to feel you come on my cock, Zara."

"No condoms."

"What did I do to deserve you?" Dragging my fingers down her flushed cheeks, I stare at her. If someone had told me a few months ago that I would have met my future wife, I would've said they were crazy. But somehow, we found our way to each other.

Shucking my boxer briefs, I settle over her. Notching myself at her entrance, I slide in slowly, savouring the feel of her heat around me. It takes everything I have not to explode inside of her. Her legs move up my hips, holding me in place as I wrap my arms around her.

I don't want any space between us. There's not a breath of air separating us. I've never been so close to a woman. I've never felt more connected to someone in my life. This woman is everything to me.

"You going to get moving there?" Zara's fingers trail down my back, fire in their wake. The slightest touch from her lights me up from the inside out.

Pulling out, I set a steady pace. Diamond hard nipples brush my chest on every stroke. My own release is racing down my spine. Need is coiling tight as I try to stave off my orgasm as Zara gets closer.

"Kiss me."

I didn't think it could get any better, but this kiss is everything. Fuck, it's the greatest kiss of my life. It's messy. It's needy. We're pouring every single emotion we're feeling into this kiss. I can't believe I thought I could do without this woman in my life.

"I'm so close, Z. You need to come." My thrusts are erratic as Zara's legs tighten around me. Whimpers escape from her lips, as I free an arm to find her clit. A ghost of a touch on that tiny bundle of nerves sets her off. Her pulsing around me is the greatest heaven I've ever known.

"Fuck." I groan out my own orgasm, pulsing deep inside her. Our lips graze each other as we savour the moment of being together again. To think, I almost lost this woman.

I go to pull out, but Zara keeps me locked in place.

"Not yet." Her hands are soft on my neck, tracing my frantic pulse. She clasps me to her, the soft pillows of her breasts the best place to land.

Dropping a kiss on the side of her chest, I slowly pull out of her. Getting up to go to the bathroom, I grab a warm washcloth to clean her up. A lazy smile dances on her lips.

"Would it be too cheesy to give you something right now?" I ask as my fingers trace circles on her stomach.

"What could you possibly need to give me after the best orgasm of my life?" Her eyes are closed, a sated look on her face.

I don't say anything, just throw on my sweats and go to grab my surprise for her. "I've been meaning to give this back to you for a few weeks now, but with everything that happened, I was a little lost."

Zara grabs my shirt and puts it on, the hem flirting with the tops of her legs. Taking the box, she pierces me with a puzzled look before taking the lid off.

"You didn't." Her hand is covering her mouth as she tearfully gazes at her violin. And not just any violin, but her most cherished one. Her mother's. "You replaced it?"

I shake my head. "No. I spoke with the company, and they were able to repair it."

Her eyes fly up to meet mine. A war of emotions is playing out in her soulful gaze. "But how? You just can't repair an instrument like this." Her hands are running over the wood and strings in a loving manner.

"I wasn't above dropping my name to get what I needed."

Setting it to the side, she stands, wrapping her arms around me. "I don't know what I did to deserve you."

"In your defence, you wouldn't have needed to replace it if you hadn't met me."

She pinches my side. "Such a smart arse."

I release my hold on her, not wanting to let her go, but wanting to hear something more. "Play for me?"

"Anything for you, my love."

I clutch my hand to my chest. I love hearing those words from her. She grabs the bow and stands before me. Light sparkles in her eyes as she starts playing. It's soulful, deep. It starts to pick up and gets more playful in the middle before taking on a sad tone again. I don't recognize it, but it touches me. I never understood music before, but Zara's love for it is infectious. She pours everything she has into the music she makes.

The piece turns happy again as Zara moves with the song. My heart catches in my chest as tears stream down Zara's cheeks. Her eyes are closed as the final note is played. There are no words for the beauty of that song. For as long as I live, I will remember this moment. Zara, looking like a goddess in my T-shirt and mussed hair, playing this beautiful song for me. And only me.

Taking the instrument from her hands, I set it down with the utmost care. Knowing the value of this violin, I don't want to take any chances with it. I pull her into my arms.

"What's the name of that song?" I want to lock in every part of this memory. I'll be old and grey and still remember this song she played for me.

"It's called James."

"James?" My brows are furrowed in confusion.

She tucks her head under my chin, wrapping her arms around me. "For the last few months, I've been trying to write music, but nothing has been coming to me. Even these last few weeks, bits and pieces were there, but always out of reach. Until today."

"And what happened today?" I squeeze her closer to me.

"Today I realized what true love is. The hard times. The fun times. The sexy times. And I get to experience all of that with the man I love."

I have to take a few steadying breaths so my emotions don't overwhelm me. "No one has ever done something so wonderful for me."

Zara turns to look at me. "You're worth it, James. Don't you ever doubt it. And if you do, I'll always be here to remind you. You're worth everything that comes with this life. Not the title. Not a way to get ahead in life, but you."

"That's music to my ears."

Chapter Twenty-Six

ZARA - TWO MONTHS LATER

I don't think I've ever been so nervous in my life. My palms are sweaty as my stomach roils.

"Is everyone ready? We'll be starting in just a few minutes." My students barely give me a second look. I can't be the only one who feels like they're going to pass out.

"Miss Cross, Prince James will introduce you, and then you'll give your speech before the show starts."

"Thank you, Alice." After everything that happened with the scandal, James and I decided I should start my own charity work. Instead of going back to school, I dove headfirst into launching my own foundation. Alice, Ellie's old advisor, was assigned to me in my new role. And with James by my side, it's gone better than I thought.

"Thank you everyone for joining us this evening. It is my great honour to introduce the head of the newest royal patronage, Lady Zara Cross."

Leaving my students on the stage, I join James out front. "Good luck. You'll do great." He gives me a peck on the cheek as I turn to face the crowd. Taking a deep breath, I start my speech.

"Thank you everyone for being here tonight. I'm thrilled to have you here at the launch of my new foundation, The Power of Music. As a former music teacher at the Hammersmith Conservatory, I know firsthand the power of music. I've seen how it can impact the lives of students and those around them." The spotlight is bright, blurring all the faces in front of me.

"My hope with The Power of Music is that we can bring music to those who wouldn't otherwise have access to it. Not just in London, but throughout the United Kingdom. And with your support, it will not only help children gain confidence, but skills to take them further in life than they ever thought possible."

Applause breaks out. "And on that note, I would like to introduce the secondary orchestra from the Hammersmith School to play for you this evening."

I leave the podium and head to the stage, the curtains now drawn. My students are all sitting, ready with their instruments. I lift my baton, and everyone sits up straight as the melody starts. All my nerves of the evening fade away. The piece is the one we were working on for the end of term concert that I never got to participate in. Even just this small event makes it worthwhile.

The students have never sounded better than they do tonight. My face is glowing as the song comes to an end. Happy, smiling faces are staring back at me. I couldn't be prouder of them than I am right now. I give them a thumbs-up as I turn to bow towards the audience. Raucous applause greets me.

One of the other conductors from the school comes on stage. As I'm off to wine and dine all of our guests, she'll take over the music portion of the evening.

Heading backstage, I let out a deep breath.

"Z! That was magnificent." James sweeps me into his arms. He swings me around, laughter bubbling out of me.

"I just don't know what to say." His eyes are alight with love and happiness. "I've never been so nervous in my life, but it went so much better than I thought."

James's lips crash down on mine. The love he gives me on a daily basis is unmatched. I love him more than life itself.

"Are you ready to get out there and win them over?" James drops his forehead to mine, his lips giving me another quick kiss.

"James." I grab him before he starts to pull me out to the main hall. "I couldn't have done this without you."

The love shining out of his eyes mirrors my own. "You did it all on your own. This is just the beginning for you, Zara." James squeezes me to him. "Everyone is going to fall in love with you. Just like I did."

I drag my fingers down his jaw, tracing over his kiss-swollen lips. "You were easy. They might be harder to win over."

"C'mon. Let's go win them over."

James

ZARA'S big night couldn't have gone better for her. The performance was incredible. Everyone was fighting to get a word with Zara. I was forgotten, and I couldn't be happier about it. And I hope the night will only get better now that we're home.

Zara hasn't officially moved in—heaven forbid two adults cohabitate——but we spend the majority of our time together.

"James. Why am I blindfolded?" I'm leading Zara through the dark gardens. There's some light from the park, but it's quiet back here.

"Just wait." My hands on her waist, I guide her towards the sunken garden surrounding the apartments here. Finding the spot, I stop and pull the blindfold off.

Her eyes go wide at the scene in front of her. A blanket is laid out before us, a bottle of champagne chilling. "What is all of this?" Awe is in her voice.

"You had this incredible night, and we need to celebrate you." I take her hand, sitting down on the blanket. I pull her between my legs as I pop open the bubbly.

"You are too much sometimes." She turns in my arms, leaning on my leg.

"Z. I am so fucking proud of you." My voice catches. It's hard to put into words just how proud of her I really am. "You shone like the brightest star tonight."

She closes her eyes as I drop a kiss on her temple. My nerves are starting to get the better of me. I take a large gulp of champagne.

"I can't wait to see how much money we raised tonight. I'm so happy that I get to do this." She looks at me, love filling her eyes. "I couldn't have done it without you."

"Bollocks. You didn't need me at all."

"Whatever you want to tell yourself." She sips at her champagne.

I take the glass from her hand, turning to face her. "Zara, there's something I want to ask you."

Her eyes widen. "Okay."

I take her hand, warm in mine in the cool London night. "I love you more than life itself. When our parents introduced us, I never thought I would fall in love with you, but I did. Hopelessly. I saw what my life would be like without you, and I never want to be without you."

Tears are glittering in her eyes.

"I want to wake up to you every day. I want to have kids with you. I want to support everything you do. I want to go to bed with you every night." I pull the ring from my pocket. Not the ring I picked out from the vault, but a ring given to me by my grandmum. "Zara Cross, will you make me the happiest man on earth and marry me?"

Zara leaps into my arms, crashing her lips down on mine. Her tongue licks at the seam of my mouth, and I open to her immediately. Love and passion swirl around us in the night.

"Is that a yes, love?"

She smacks me in the chest. "Of course, yes!"

I pull the ring out of the box and slide it on her finger. "James, it's absolutely gorgeous."

She holds her hand out in front of her face.

"It's from my grandmum. It was what Granddad proposed with." The ring isn't extravagant but has three stones set on a gold band. Nothing over-the-top, but perfect for Zara.

"If we have half the love they do, we're going to be just fine."

"That we are, love. That we are."

Epilogue

I hardly slept a wink last night. Butterflies threatened to overtake me anytime I thought about today. It is the day people have been looking forward to since James and I announced our engagement a few short months ago.

"You doing alright?" Charlotte's voice brings me back to the hotel room we're occupying before the service.

"Little nervous." My voice is quiet as I run my hands over my dress.

"Any second thoughts?" Marnie's voice is filled with laughter. "If he really isn't up to snuff,"—she waggles her pinkie in my direction—"you can back out now."

"Gross. Things I don't want to know about my brother." Ellie's pacing the room, swinging her new bundle of joy in her arms.

"You look stunning. James isn't going to know what hit him." Charlotte clasps my hand in hers, settling my nerves. "I don't know how anyone will ever compare to you."

I look in the mirror. The high-necked embroidered gown with cap sleeves is perfect. It hugs every curve before the skirt fans out around my hips. The veil covering my face has elements from all the countries of the common-wealth woven in. The tiara, loaned to me by the Queen, completes the ensemble. In short, I look like a Princess.

I don't know how my designer managed to create this masterpiece in a matter of a few months, but it's every-thing I dreamed it would be. James and I moved fast. After he proposed to me after the launch of my charity, we thought a winter wedding would be perfect. We had joked we'd be getting married fast when this whole arrangement started. And now, we didn't want to wait another second to start our lives together.

A knock at the door has everyone quieting down. The wedding coordinator pops her head in the suite. "The carriages are here. Are you ready?"

"We'll be down in a moment."

She looks down at her clipboard. "We need to leave in five minutes to stay on schedule." Her lips are drawn tight.

"They won't start without her. We'll be down in a moment." The Queen dismisses her. "Girls, would you mind heading downstairs? I'd like a moment alone with Zara."

"You look beautiful. Don't let her scare you off," Ellie whispers in my ear as she follows Charlotte and Marnie out the door. It shuts with a soft click.

"I know we need to get downstairs, but I didn't want you to leave without giving you a small something." She pulls a long, velvet box out of her bag that sits on the bed.

Opening it, I find a diamond halo bracelet in white gold. A gasp escapes my throat. "This is beautiful."

"May I?" She takes it out as I extend my hand to her. "My father gave it to me on my wedding, and I would like you to have it today."

Tears glisten in my eyes as I try to hold back my emotions of receiving such a thoughtful gift. "I will cherish this. Thank you." I spin my wrist, the light catching the diamonds from the sun shining in through the window.

"Thank you for being the woman my son needs." She cups my cheeks. "I know most people don't know how the two of you met, but you are the epitome of strength and grace. It will be many years to come, but you will be the Queen James needs at his side when the time comes. And I rest easy knowing that you two have each other to take on all that this life throws at you."

A single tear trickles out, carving a hot path down my cheek. "Thank you for saying that. I love James with all that I am. Whatever is thrown at us, I'll be ready." Hearing those words from her means more than I could ever say.

She sucks in a deep breath, trying to calm her own emotions. "Come now. We best get downstairs. I don't want to be blamed for your makeup being messed up on a day like today."

I let out a bark of laughter. "She is rather scary, isn't she?"

"All good wedding planners are. Now, let's get you to the church."

"YOU READY, DARLING?" Dad's voice is barely audible over the cheers as I step out of the carriage at the entrance to the abbey. The ride from the hotel to the church took no time at all. My cheeks hurt from the smile pasted on my face. The wedding planner told me hundreds of times that any break in my face would be captured on film for the entire world to see.

"As I'll ever be."

I give a small wave to everyone outside the church, and cheers explode from the crowd. I take Dad's hand as we prepare to walk into the church. Marnie's behind me, fluffing out the back of my dress. She gives me a wink as we start to walk inside. The noise of the crowd dies out as soon as the heavy wooden doors close. As the music starts, everyone stands.

I don't recognize half the people here. Nods and bows are directed my way as we make our way down the aisle. We practised this only last night, but it didn't feel so endless then. When we make it to the archway, dissecting the church, James finally comes into view. He's wearing his military uniform today, his hair slicked back.

He's never looked more perfect to me than he does right now. I start to walk faster, but Dad slows me down. "You'll get there soon enough, darling." I turn to face him and see tears in his eyes. "Just let me have one more moment with my daughter before the entire world gets you."

I stop, right there in the middle of the aisle, and wrap my arms around him. "I'll always be your little girl."

He squeezes me a little harder before pulling back. "I know your mother would love James." His voice breaks a little, as I hold on just a little tighter.

"Come now, time to get you to your groom. He's looking a little antsy." James is rocking side to side as I catch his eye. He gives me a smile.

Linking my arm through my dad's, we make it to James. "Take care of each other." Dad clasps James's hand before giving me a kiss on the cheek. He goes to take his seat as James takes my hand.

"You think you could speed it up next time? I've been waiting here all day."

"Sorry. I'll be sure to hurry it along the next time we

get married." I squeeze his hand as the minister calls everyone to be seated.

Now to make it through the next hour without fainting and I'll be okay.

James

"HOW DO YOU FEEL, my darling wife?" We finally have a quiet moment on the dance floor. It's been a whirlwind of a day. From the moment I saw Zara walking towards me, I've been in a state of pure bliss. She looks like an angel, unlike anything I've ever seen before in my life.

From the carriage ride through the city, to our very public kiss on the balcony with people screaming from the streets, it's been nothing but insanity. But insanity of the best kind.

"Hmm, I'm kind of hoping we get to leave on our honeymoon soon."

I twirl a loose lock of hair around my finger. "Oh yeah?"

She tucks her face into my neck, dropping a kiss there. "We've been around people all day. I'm ready for it to just be the two of us."

I spin her away from me, pulling her back in a dip. "Only a little while longer, my love."

I haven't left her side today. After a huge party for all the foreign dignitaries, we came to Clarence House for a smaller gathering of family and friends. One that I'm ready to cut and run from.

"It has been a pretty spectacular day." Zara is glowing.

"That it has, my beautiful wife." I can't get enough of it. Calling Zara my wife. I never thought the day would come, but here I am. I'd lay down my life for this woman.

"Excuse me. Prince James. Princess Zara. The fireworks are about to begin and then you can take your leave." Charles is at our shoulder. Zara beams at him.

"Thank you." I tuck her hand in mine, following the guests outside. "I believe that is the first time someone has called you princess."

"You would be correct." She wraps her arm around my waist as Marnie hands her the fur stole to keep warm. The temperature has dropped, but it cools my heated skin. Everywhere we've been today, people upon people have been congratulating us and wishing us well.

As we step out onto the balcony, fireworks burst into the dark February sky. Oohs and aahs echo around us. Pulling Zara in front of me, I wrap her in my arms, resting my chin on her shoulder. She leans into my touch.

"You know, I never imagined my wedding day would be like this."

"Oh yeah?" I ghost my lips along her ear. It's been too long since I've been able to touch her how I want. We've spent the last few nights apart while the final preparations were done for the wedding. Several people told us it would be crass if people saw either one of us leaving the other's home in the morning. We knew it, but we didn't like it.

"I thought it would be just a few close family and friends. Nothing broadcast all over the world for everyone to see."

"Any regrets?"

"Not a one." My heart picks up as the fireworks continue to explode across the London sky. "This was better than I ever could have dreamed."

"I never thought I'd get married, but then you came along. I couldn't have wished for a better person if I tried."

She laughs, the sound warming me from the inside out. "Not bad for an arranged marriage, huh?"

No, not bad at all.

The End

Bonus Scene

"And you enjoyed our country, Your Highness? I'm sorry it was such a short visit."

It's still a shock to hear myself called that.

"Sweden is a beautiful country. I hope we can come back and see more of it one day, King Anders." Our first official state visit as husband and wife was to Sweden.

He chuckles at me. "Did I tell you your husband once called me Prince Anders?"

I smile at the memory. I was freaking out over marrying James and he told me about this slip-up. "He has. It must be something in the air here. You and your wife both look younger than James and I."

He claps my hand that is looped through his arm. "You know just what to say to this old man."

"I have so enjoyed meeting you on this trip." We approach James and the queen, awaiting our arrival at the front of the palace. "I only hope you can come visit us in England soon."

"I hope so. I've always enjoyed my time there. Even spent some time in uni there."

"I don't think I knew that." James and the queen are laughing at something as we approach them.

"Ah, yes. Got into quite a bit of trouble. But I won't regale you with those stories. Not appropriate for mixed company."

"And did you two have a nice visit?" The queen drops a kiss on Anders' cheek as James takes me in his arms.

"It was quite lovely. Zara is a lovely representative of England."

I smile at the two, before looking at James. "It was a wonderful visit. I only wish we could stay longer."

James gives me his most winning smile. "The life of royalty. We have a lot awaiting us at home."

Anders shakes James' hand. "I only hope our paths cross again soon."

"King Anders. It's always a pleasure."

We are escorted out to the idling car, waving at the press as I slide across the seat. "Ready to get home?" James pulls me into his side as we're swept away through Stockholm traffic.

"So ready." I kick my heels off, leaning into James' touch. "I'd much rather have a three-week tour, as opposed to two days. They pack too much into our schedule."

James claims my lips in a kiss. He keeps me close to him as he drops his forehead to mine. "But at least we have a few days to ourselves when we get home before your event this weekend."

"A few days to ourselves?" I push back from James. "I'll be working to make sure everything goes off without a hitch."

James tucks a loose strand of hair behind my ear. "As if it will be anything but a success." His warm lips find my neck.

"You're biased."

His lips trail up my neck, nibbling on my jaw. "Yes. I happen to think anything my wife does is a success. But I know you. Everything will be perfect."

"As long as I don't get sick, everything will be perfect."

James' hand rubs over my belly. "I still can't believe we're going to be parents. I don't think I'm ready."

I drape my hand over his, keeping it there. "Just don't think about how we're raising the future monarch. I keep panicking about how many ways we could screw this little one up."

A tender look crosses James' face. "There's no way this child will screw up, especially with you being their mum." His lips move up my neck. "Do you know how gorgeous you're going to be with a bump?"

I smile, letting his words wash over me. We found out a few weeks ago we were expecting. The morning sickness is more like all day sickness. Thankfully today it wasn't bad as we met with Sweden's king and queen. I can only imagine how it would've gone over if I'd gotten sick at the luncheon.

"Do you know how wonderful you're going to be with this one?" I flit my gaze to him. My heart swells with love for this man. And to think, I wanted nothing to do with this man when I first met him.

The car comes to a stop. "We can't already be at the airport, can we?" It seems like we only just went around the block.

A grin splits James' face. "Have a little surprise for you, love." James pulls me out of the car, in what looks like the back of the palace.

"Don't we have to get home?"

"Zara, love. We can take as long as we want. Perk of being first in line." James winks at me, and butterflies swarm my stomach. "Now, follow me."

Large walls covered in ivy surround us. The sky is bright blue overhead. Walking around a corner, James pulls me to the front of a lush garden.

Colour explodes as far as the eye can see. The fragrant scent of flowers hangs heavy in the air.

"Are we allowed to be here?" My eyes move fast, taking in everything around me.

"By special permission of the king." James gives me his elbow, and I link my arm through his. "I know how much you love the gardens at home, so I thought we could take a minute, just the two of us, before me left."

"You really are Prince Charming, you know that?" I rest my head on his shoulder as he guides us through the park. A small stream leads the way. Fountains dot the gravel pathway.

"I have to do something to keep you around."

I squeeze James' bicep, pulling him to a stop. Bees and butterflies float around us. "You should know by now that you don't need to do anything to keep me around other than just being yourself."

"God, I love you." James slants his mouth over mine, taking me in a heated kiss. Even after two years together, it still feels like the first time. When my stomach fluttered in my chest and my heart pulled towards his.

"You know we probably shouldn't do this in the middle of palace grounds." I pepper a few soft kisses on James' mouth. "They probably have cameras back here. Don't want to soil our good name."

James wraps his arms around my waist, holding me close. "You raise an excellent point, but you're irresistible." He tucks a stray strand of hair behind my ear, fingers lingering on my neck. "Besides, we won't get many more moments like this...just you and me."

"We have several months before the baby comes. There will be plenty of moments between now and then."

"Not when we're in Sweden. Sneaking around the palace grounds."

"James Henry! You did not sneak us in here!" My voice is high, as James gives me a sheepish look.

He just laughs at me. "You're too easy sometimes, love."

I smack him on the shoulder before nestling into his side. "You're lucky I like you so much."

James' arm wraps around my shoulder as we stand in the gardens. "I am lucky. To have you. This baby. We have a pretty incredible life."

That we do. That we do.

Read on for a sneak peek of Royal Relations!

Sneak Peek

CHARLOTTE

"You made it!" Ellie wraps her arms around me as I rush into the sitting room at the palace.

"Sorry I'm late. Lost track of time working."

"I'm just happy you were able to come." Ellie loops her arm through mine and pulls me farther into the crowded room.

"I thought you said this was going to be a small celebration."

Ellie rolls her eyes. "Sean's mum planned everything, and then my mum sort of took over."

"As she does. But it does look pretty good in here."

Flowers decorate all the surfaces in the family room in the palace. A table is overflowing with gifts in the corner. "Presents? I thought you didn't want any."

I turn my gaze back to Ellie. Her pink hair is braided around her head. She's wearing a long, white dress that clings to her baby bump. She's absolutely glowing.

"I didn't. Sean and I need nothing, but everyone brought something." Ellie's eyes shift to find Sean. He's standing next to someone I haven't seen before, but the stranger's eyes pull me in. Bright blue eyes that are filled with laughter. White teeth hidden behind plump lips.

"Who is that—-" I'm cut off.

"Charlotte. I'm so pleased you could join us today." Aunt Katherine, better known as the Queen, pulls me in for a hug.

"I just can't believe Ellie is having a baby." I squeeze Ellie's shoulder. As cousins near the same age, she's been one of my closest friends for as long as I can remember. "I can't wait to meet this little baby."

"I just wish we knew what she was having." Katherine gives Ellie a look.

"Mum. You'll meet them soon enough," Ellie reminds her.

"Katherine. Stop bothering Eleanor." My mum appears at my side. "Hello, darling."

"Hi, Mum." I give her a quick side hug as a server with champagne walks by.

"Just you wait until Charlotte begins having kids. It will drive you just as crazy."

I choke over my sip of champagne at Aunt Katherine's words. "I'm not even dating someone. Let's not talk about that."

"Better you than me," Ellie laughs.

"I'm sure they'll be asking when baby number two will pop out before long."

The mystery man crosses my view, talking to James and Zara. My mum and Aunt Katherine get carried away into a conversation about the baby and who will have another child first. A conversation only mums can have.

"Who's that talking with James and Zara?" I whisper over the top of my drink to Ellie. No need to broadcast who I'm looking at.

"Who, Pierce? That's Sean's brother."

It's as if he hears his name. Pierce turns and looks over at Ellie and me. A small smile plays on his lips. Flutters erupt deep in my belly, something I haven't felt in a long time.

Before I can make my way over to him, my attention is pulled away and he's gone.

I need to meet this man.

Read Royal Relations in Kindle Unlimited today!

Author Note

Book four is officially out in the world! I absolutely loved writing James and Zara and hope you love them as much as I do!

It never ceases to amaze me how amazing the romance community is. All the love and support from this community keeps me going! And to my Accountability Tribe… Norma and AK…you two are amazing and keep me laughing on the days where I want to cry!

To the best beta readers…Audrey and Tara…thank you for helping me make this book what it is! To my ARC team…thank you for all the love and support you give me.

And to all the amazing readers out there…thank you for picking up my book and helping make all my author dreams come true!

xo, Emily

About the Author

After winning a Young Author's Award in second grade, Emily Silver was destined to be a writer. She loves writing strong heroines and the swoony men who fall for them.

A lover of all things romance, Emily started writing books set in her favorite places around the world. As an avid traveler, she's been to all seven continents and sailed around the globe.

When she's not writing, Emily can be found sipping cocktails on her porch, reading all the romance she can get her hands on and planning her next big adventure!

Find her on social media to stay up to date on all her adventures and upcoming releases!

Also by Emily Silver

The Ainsworth Royals

Royal Reckoning

Reckless Royal

Royal Relations

Royal Roots

Royal Ties

The Love Abroad Series

An Icy Infatuation

A French Fling

A Sydney Surprise

The Denver Mountain Lions

Roughing The Kicker

Pass Interference

Sideline Infraction

Illegal Contact

The Big Game

Off the Deep End — A standalone, MM sports romance

Get all my titles now:

www.ingramcontent.com/pod-product-compliance
Lightning Source LLC
Chambersburg PA
CBHW030812210726
48290CB00002B/552